CALLING PARADISE

JACQUELINE DAUDET

This book is dedicated to
Tim Nygard, who has always believed in me.
"You're in Paradise now"

ONE

THE WAVES ONCE CALM were now poised for destruction, individually crashing along the shoreline with full power. The tiny wooden house stood high above the ocean floor on its pillars, bracing itself for the impending doom.

Inside there was life, a family of four, who prepared themselves for the one final blow that would destroy their very existence. Each of the children were given a tiny metal box and were told not in a voice that you and I would use to communicate, but telepathically, that they were to retrieve a photograph, along with their most cherished valuables.

They were given a tiny red capsule and told to lie on their bunk beds. The small boy looked deep into his father's eyes and was told that you will know when it's time to swallow. The boy understood. He gathered his belongings and lay on his bed. He gave his mother and sister one last look, and then closed his eyes.

Outside their world was coming to an end. The tropical landscape was crumbling into the sea. Without needing to confirm the devastation, they could see that a large part of the mountain was about to crush their home. All at once in unison, the family placed their pills into their mouths and closed their eyes. In an instant the sea reclaimed its rightful ownership, and nothing remained.

Samantha Woods awoke suddenly as she most often did when she had this recurring dream. She lay in her bed and closed her eyes, replaying each scene so as not to forget every detail. When she felt that it was deeply embedded in her mind, she decided it was time to get up and start her day. She reached for her robe and draped it over her slim body. First and foremost on her list was a cup of coffee, then a refreshing swim. She walked down the stairs and into the kitchen. Once her coffee was prepared, she took her cup outside into her topical garden paradise. She sat on her lanai and listened to the sweet songs of the birds in her garden.

Beyond her yard there was in all its splendor the enchanting Pacific Ocean. She sipped her coffee and listened to the symphony of the waves crashing on the shoreline. She felt very fortunate to be living in such a tropical paradise. Living on the island had always been a childhood dream of hers. Walking around her yard she noticed several small lizards frolicking from one hibiscus leaf to another. They were adorable as she watched them go into their invisible stance. Frozen with one eye focused on your every move. She backed up slowly, but her motion caused them to scurry off into the dense protective cover of the leaves.

Taking her final sip of coffee, she was now done and ready for a quick dip into the sun-splashed warm waves before she was off to work. Walking back into the house she placed her coffee cup on to the kitchen counter and grabbed her swim suit and towel from the laundry room. Once changed it was out the door and down to the beach.

Standing knee-deep in water by the shore, she scanned the horizon and watched the waves heading towards her. A large wave caught her off guard slamming her body with such force that it threw her back on to the shore. Another wave followed close behind. Once it passed, she jumped back into the warm azure waters and swam along the shoreline. Her neighbors were out waxing down their surf boards—all surfer dudes.

She smiled to herself. Surfing was something that she wanted to try, one day she would when she could gather up the courage. Finding a teacher would be no problem as her dudes had expressed their eagerness quite frequently to teach her. Everyone on the island apparently knew how to surf. Water sports were what everyone did as children, along with learning the importance of respecting all life.

She had lived in Hawaii for five years and had become very well accustomed to the Hawaiian ways. All things on the island had life and were treated with great respect. The ocean was a powerful force. Although serene, it created life but could just as easily destroy life at any given moment. Beginning to tire, she decided to turn around and swim to the shore in front of her house. For fun, she body surfed. Standing knee-deep in water she crouched down, turned her head and waited for the precise moment when a wave was in sight.

Just as the wave drew near and the water rose, she bent down and stretched her arms out in front of her as if ready for a dive.

Once the conditions were right, she pushed herself off letting the wave carry her on to the warm golden sand. The receding waters were forcibly reclaiming her body back into its hidden depths. She stood up before the next wave was about to hurl itself on to the shore. Turning just in time to see the large wave crest and disperse on to the wet sand. The warmth of the froth tickled her ankles as she ran up on to the beach. Her fun for the morning would have to wait, getting to work was now on her mind.

Sam showered and dressed, which consisted of a pair of shorts, tank top, hat, an oversized men's shirt and hiking boots. Grabbing her back pack and a bottle of water she headed towards the door when her phone rang. She hesitated whether to answer it. Who would call her on her land line? Throwing down her pack she picked up the receiver.

"Hello. Yes, this is Samantha Woods" She didn't recognize the voice.

"Who is this?"

He mentioned his name and suddenly she was speechless. All she could do was listen to the distant voice, nothing registered; her mind was unfocused. The voice on the other end grew increasingly louder, snapping her back to reality.

"Yes. I remember you. Wow! It's been a long time." His name was Michael North, a man she had once dated in college, at a time that was as faded as the last rays of the setting sun.

"Where are you?" she asked.

"I'm here in Maui at the airport."

"What? Why?"

"I would like to see you. Would it be possible for us to meet?"

She paused reluctant to give him an answer.

"Well, no—I'm just on my way out to work."

"Oh. Then when would be a good time?"

"Well, I don't know."

"Oh, I see. When will you be off?" He was persistent.

"Umm, it depends, there's no real set time so—"

"I would really like to see you. Can you please make an exception? It's not every day that I travel to Maui to see an old friend."

"OK then. I can meet you at 5 o'clock."

"That will be great Samantha, thank you! So where should we meet?"

"Where are you staying?"

"I'm staying in Kihei at the Days Inn do you know

where that is?"

"Yes actually I do. There's a lounge just down the street from you that's close by—the Tiki Lounge. It's walking distance from where you are staying."

"OK."

"It's just actually north of you through town."

"I'll find it. See you there at around five."

She hung up the phone, grabbed her back pack and walked out the door to her jeep that was parked in the driveway. She started it up and backed on to the road, thinking what just happened?

Why after fifteen years was he calling her? And how did he find her phone number? Admittedly she was curious, but her curiosity would have to wait, for today she had to travel to the Iao Valley, which wasn't a long drive from her home in Lahaina, about 40 minutes if the traffic flowed. She turned on to Front Street, which was always filled with tourists and made a slow go of it. Once she turned right on to Keniu Street, it was just on to Highway 30 and a relatively smooth flow until she reached the Valley.

TWO

H IS FLIGHT HAD JUST landed from San Francisco and he was hoping to meet with Samantha before looking for a place to stay. Secretly he wanted her to supply him with the accommodations. Unfortunately, the call was not as well received as he had hoped. He checked his wallet, which didn't contain an abundance of funds, since he had spent most of his money to get to Maui. The amount available on his Visa card would only cover his stay for a week; after that he was on his own. Walking to the front of the airport he noticed several cabs waiting eagerly to take excited tourists to their destinations. Mike was approached by a short stocky man.

"Cab Mister?"

"Yes. How much to Kihei?

"About sixty dollars." Great thought Mike, there goes my food money.

"Well, OK. Thank you."

The cabbie picked up his luggage and loaded it into the trunk.

"Where to?" asked the cabbie.

"I'm staying in Kihei at the Days Inn."

"Is this your first time here in Maui?"

"Yes, it is." nodded Mike as he looked out of the window.

"Well I'm sure you will enjoy your stay." The cabbie glanced into his rear view mirror. "Yes. I'm hoping I will."

The cab took a turn on to the highway. "So where are you from?" asked the cabbie.

"San Francisco." Mike wasn't in a talkative mood and had hoped that if he gave one-word answers, he could keep his conversation to a minimum.

"Oh San Francisco, I've heard it's very nice there. I've never been but I do have an uncle who lives there. Yeah, he's a distant uncle. Whereabouts in San Francisco are you from?"

"Napa Valley."

"Oh, my uncle is in Oakland. Do you know where that is?"

"Yes, I do."

"Oh, I see."

His mother worked at a restaurant in Fisherman's Wharf; her wages were bare minimum but with an added bonus at the height of the tourist season she made up for it in tips. His father worked, when he did, in odd jobs that would only last for a short period due to his drinking. Michael would often come to blows with his father, always defending and protecting his mother. He never understood why she put up with him as much as she did. He supposed her being Catholic and believing in the sanctity of marriage gave her the strength to endure. He missed his mother every single day. Both of his parents were killed in the 1989 Oakland earthquake. A customer had given his mother two free tickets to the World Series game and they were on the bridge when it hit.

Oakland, thought Mike, brought back a flood of memories. He was asked to go with his mother but opted out when he was called into work at the last minute. He always felt that he should have been with her, maybe he could have done something to save her. His mother would have been proud of him being the first in his family to go to university.

He had saved up enough money by working in several odd jobs until he was able to afford the tuition at the University of San Francisco. He enrolled in the archaeology program, which was his passion at that time, and that is where he first met Samantha. He fell madly in love with her at first sight. Her upbringing was one of family unity and wealth. Her family was a big producer of wine from the Napa Valley region, old money—the acreage had been passed down through generations. Her parents wanted her to take over the business, but she had other plans. Despite her father's disapproval she enrolled in archaeology, which was her passion.

Mike was amazed at how they still managed to be

very compatible, even though they were from completely different backgrounds. She was his ideal woman, tall, slim with eyes that were the color of copper. Her soft shoulder-length chestnut brown hair was a stunning contrast to her eyes. Samantha was a very outdoorsy woman who took her studies of archaeology very seriously, becoming an honor student. Unlike him, who just barely got by.

"We're here!" said the cabbie as he pulled into the hotel driveway.

"How much?" asked Mike.

"That will be sixty-five dollars." Mike pulled out his wallet and paid the man with a small tip.

"Mahalo," said the cabbie as he unloaded Mike's luggage.

"Mahalo," replied Mike.

Mike picked up his luggage and walked into the lobby of the hotel.

"Aloha," said a young girl from behind the front desk.

"Hello." Mike decided that he would repeat her greeting.

"Aloha. I have a reservation."

"Very good Sir, and your name?"

"Mike. Michael North."

"One moment please. I'll just confirm your reservation.

"Oh yes. There you are, one bedroom with a double bed and a kitchenette."

"Yes, that's right."

"And you will be staying with us for a week, correct?"

"Right."

"Good. Here are your keys and you are in room number 215."

"Would you like some help with your luggage?"

"No. That's quite all right I can manage."

"Very good, Sir. The elevator is just down the hall and, on your left. Mahalo and hope you enjoy your stay."

"Mahalo," said Mike, who was beginning to enjoy the Hawaiian language. He entered the elevator and pushed the button for the 2nd floor. A young couple also entered the elevator, pressing the 2nd floor. They immediately embraced—must be on their honeymoon thought Mike. The elevator stopped on the second and he waited till they exited. Mike picked up his luggage and began to look for his room. He turned right as the numbers were beginning to ascend. Finding his room number at a corner suite he unlocked the door and entered.

The room was not spectacular; however, it was clean and comfortable. Throwing down his bags he walked over towards the balcony and pulled the drapes open. It was a fabulous view of the ocean front and the balcony had lounge chairs and a table. Satisfied with his accommodations he started to unpack and change into his swimming trunks. It was still early until his meeting with Samantha, so perhaps a swim. But a drink first, of course, after all it was happy hour, well not quite, but what the heck he was in Hawaii.

Reaching into his carry-on bag he pulled out a bottle of gin. It would just have to be with ice until he got some mixers. Opening the fridge and looking into the freezer he found a full ice cube tray. He filled his glass with gin and added several ice cubes.

Taking a sip, he walked out on to his balcony, scanned the horizon of the immense Pacific Ocean. Breathtaking! Mike took a last sip, and then made another one that went down too smoothly. Looking at his watch he realized that he had a lot of time to kill; it was only 12:30 p.m. He walked back out on to the balcony, sat down and decided to just relax and take in the beauty that surrounded him. Perhaps a swim in a bit.

Taking another sip, he placed his glass down on the table and closed his eyes. Before he could doze off there was a knock on the door. Who could that be? He wasn't expecting anyone. He walked towards the door and turned the knob when suddenly it swung open throwing him back. There in front of him stood a large Hawaiian, whom he had never seen before.

"Hello Mike," a voice seemed to be coming from nowhere until the Hawaiian stepped aside.

"Tom! What are you doing here?"

"Why visiting you, of course." They walked into the room.

"So Mike, how have you been?"

"Please sit down, relax," said the little man.

Mike sat down and Tom sat beside him as the Hawaiian stood by his side.

"Mike, Mike! We did have a heck of a time trying to find you. Hawaii? Why Hawaii?"

"I needed a vacation away from you. What are you doing here?"

"Away from me? Aw, come on Mike, we're old friends don't be like that."

"You're not a friend Tom, you're just business."

"My words exactly, and it's my business to collect the money you owe me."

"You'll get your money. I told you."

"Oh, I know I will one way or another. Hey, I'm getting a little thirsty here. What are you drinking?"

"Gin over ice." Tom motioned for the giant to fix him a drink. The Hawaiian returned with the drink.

"Now that's better. Now Mike, this is the second time that you promised to pay up."

"Tom, I have every intention of paying you."

"Really? I would totally think that's bullshit you know. Then why did you run away to Hawaii?"

"I have a lead. If it pays off, then you'll get the money I owe you with interest."

"Yeah, so what is the lead?"

"I can't tell you."

Tom took a drink.

"Yeah...you can't hey?"

"No, not yet." Tom stood up and nodded at the Hawaiian who walked towards Mike. His expression was emotionless.

"Tom, really you have to believe me."

"Well Mike, I hope you're telling the truth because I hate to be made a fool!"

"Tom, really I do have a plan."

"Again, what is your plan?" Tom walked behind the giant, nodding.

"I can't say right now," but before Mike could say another word the giant grabbed his arm and twisted it behind his back. Mike yelled out.

"Damn it! You'll get your money!"

The giant backed off.

"You better believe I will by the end of the week or you're shark bait!"

Tom poured himself a shot of gin and downed it.

"Damn you man! Consider this your last chance—by the end of week, you got it?" Tom and the Hawaiian slammed the door behind them.

Mike was now alone. He made himself a stiff drink minus the ice and downed it. Then another and another. How did they ever find him? He had taken every precaution to lose them on the mainland. He was certain that his troubles were far behind him, but now they were back with a vengeance. He had to come up with fifty thousand dollars and in a hurry.

THREE

THE SCENERY WAS SPECTACULAR with its lush tropical rainforest as far as the eye could see. She was gaining elevation at 1,000 feet above sea level. The humidity seemed denser than below; perhaps it was the thinning air.

Once Sam reached the top, she pulled into the parking lot, which was as close as she was going to get—the rest of the way would be on foot. She grabbed her backpack and a bottle of water, took a drink and then locked up the jeep. It was an easy walk at first as the pathway was paved, but after that it was an unmarked trek to the site.

The site was situated at the base of the Iao Needle, which was surrounded by lush growth. As she walked along the path, she imaged how it would have looked back in the day when no tourists would be passing her by.

Perhaps the sounds of drumming and chanting could be heard off in the distance. Natives would be talking amongst themselves possibly getting ready for the battle. The great battle that ensued in the year 1790 that had King Kamehameha conquer Kalanikupule and Maui's army, uniting the Hawaiian Islands. The mystery of the burial grounds of King Kamehameha still remains a mystery. She fantasized about finding his remains—that would be the discovery of the century!

As she was admiring the verdant flora, the thought of meeting up with Mike entered her mind; she wasn't sure if she wanted to see him at all. They had a past and maybe their past was better left buried.

Once she emerged from the bend, there stood the Hawaiian Council waiting for her. The dig was on an ancient burial ground and the Council had to be present to show their respect for their land and ancestors. Sam had met with Chief Elder Makani on several occasions as part of her work had often brought them together.

She had a deep respect for him and on occasion he could be quite humorous in a rather staunch way. He was a large man standing at six foot four. When his dark eyes looked into yours, they were hypnotic, reaching into your very soul, searching for the truth of your existence.

Makani had come from a long line of elders, reaching back to the ancient ways. His knowledge surpassed any knowledge taught in history books, knowledge that consisted of this world as well as the unseen.

"Aloha. Morning Makani; it's nice to see you."

"Aloha. Morning, it's been a while."

Sam and Makani shared an old Hawaiian traditional Ha (breath) by placing her forehead upon his and drawing breath from each-other. She felt honored to share such a precious gift with an elder.

"It is nice to see you my friend," said Makani. "You haven't been at our sites as often as before."

"No, Makani, not as much anymore; it seems that the majority of archaeological work is more about land development rather than remote burial sites."

"Yes, I know," said Makani, nodding his head in agreement.

"It's a sad thing when the old buildings are being replaced for bigger and what they perceive as better."

"So true, Makani, there seems to be little respect or interest for the past."

Makani placed his hands in prayer.

"How I long for the old ways," he said.

"Yes, I remember even in the seventies how quaint these islands were with the old little beach houses that dotted the seaside."

"Exactly. Just from a short time ago, see how things have changed. Let's walk. I'll show you where we found it—only in knowing from the past can we truly know the future."

"Oh, I agree with you there. These Hawaiian Islands are rich in history. One might consider all of the islands as an ancestral heritage site."

"Yes, Sam I would love it if it could be so." Makani smiled. "We could tell everyone who doesn't respect our culture and land to get the heck off." He laughed.

Sam smiled. "Oh, I'm sure that would go over well."

Makani stopped in front of a mound of freshly unearthed soil and reached down and pointed to a small shinny object that looked like metal or tin.

"We found this. What do you think it is?"

"Hmm, odd. Why would there be metal at this site?"

"I'm not too sure, but this is strange."

"How deep into the ground was it?"

"We found it within, I'd say about five feet."

"Has it been moved?"

"No, it's in the exact same spot? We thought it was best not to move it until you arrived."

"Mahalo, I'll just document the find."

Sam removed her camera and her tools that consisted of a round-edged shovel and gloves from her pack. Lowing herself into the pit, she took several pictures before carefully digging around the object and removing it. As the soil loosened and cascaded down the face of the pit, she noticed a small off-white object.

She reached for her brush in her back pocket and gently sweep away the soil, being careful not to damage it in anyway. Once it was exposed, she could see that it was a small bone. She continued to dig around it, but nothing else was found. She placed the box in a zip lock baggie and another for the small bone.

"Makani!" Sam shouted.

"Yes, what is it?"

Sam extended her arm so that Makani could help her out of the pit.

"I found this box as well as what looks like a small bone. I'm guessing from a child."

Makani inspected it. "Interesting. I think you could be right. It looks like a bone from an index finger perhaps?"

"I'm impressed Makani; you are absolutely right. It's actually called the distal phalanx."

"I knew that!"

"I'm sure you did." Sam smiled.

Makani had known enough about artifacts as he made it his business to be well informed in all things that were found at the sites. Sam called out to one of her student assistants.

"Lani!"

"Yes?" A young girl in her early twenties approached Sam.

"Can you please make sure that these objects are catalogued? I would like to take them with me for further study." Sam handed her the objects.

"OK, I'll be right back with them."

Makani turned towards Sam.

"So, have you found anyone yet?"

"What do you mean? Oh, no, and I'm not looking."

"Beautiful girl like you should have someone in your life."

"Oh, Makani I do."

"You do? Who?"

"It's you." She grabbed his arm, and Makani laughed.

"You will have to get an OK from my wife; she might still want me."

"Oh, I'm sure she'll want to keep you all to herself; you're a good man. You know what Makani? You can be my work husband. How's that?" she said, laughing.

"Work husband? I think she would be OK with that. You know I really like that. OK, that's what we are. I'll have to tell her that."

They both laughed.

Lani returned with the artifacts.

"Mahalo Lani, can you please continue to dig in the pit where we found these objects; just in case I've missed something."

"I will," nodded Lani.

"Well I'm going."

Sam placed the tin and bone separately into her pack so as not to disturb each artifact.

"Why so early? Don't tell me you have a date?"

"OK, I won't tell you."

"Sam, who is he?"

"Just an old friend."

"Oh, really now—"

"Makani really he's just an old friend—why is my husband jealous?"

Makani placed his arm around her. "Me jealous?

Never—well maybe almost never."

"Makani, you know I love you." Sam kissed him on his cheek.

"I've got to run now. Give my Aloha to your wife, first wife—ha ha!"

"I will Sam. Blessings. See you?"

"Soon I promise. I'll call you and let you know what I find, my husband," Sam said, laughing.

"I can't wait, wife."

Makani laughed, and then turned to see one of his tribal members standing behind him.

"Makani?"

"Yes?"

"She's not your wife, is she?"

Makani burst into laughter. "Come on let's go do some digging."

Sam unlocked her jeep and threw her pack on to the passenger seat. She looked at her watch—2:30. She still had time to pick up a few things at Safeway before meeting Mike. Well that is if she decided to go. Anyway, she needed a few things.

She left the parking lot just as a bus was unloading a swarm of tourists, perfect timing. Driving down the winding road that connected to the freeway, the traffic started to back up as it was now rush hour.

The island highway definitely needed an expansion, since cars were often at a standstill. She remembered a time when there was a horrific accident and no one could move for hours. People didn't get home until late at night or not home at all. Thankfully, this wasn't the case today, just congestion.

Glancing at her dash it was three o'clock and she wasn't even at the halfway mark. Well, if she was late, then undoubtedly that would be a sign not to go. Safeway was still one of her stops. The vehicles finally started to move, far below the speed limit, nevertheless, they were moving.

Her mind switched from the amazing find on to Mike. She had moved on and had made quite a life for herself. Living in Maui was a yearning like she had never felt in her whole life—an indescribable need to be a part of this land. It was in her blood. With loving the islands as much as she did, she had an understanding of the age old concept of longing for your homeland.

It's the unseen force, the mana or power that lives in every collective entity of spirit that forms these islands and its people. Once you understand, its essence captures you never letting you go.

Sam felt a kinship, and even though she wasn't native every part of her being felt that she was. It was amazing that she had a passion for archaeology, which enabled her to learn so much more of the ancient ways.

She was proud of her accomplishments and her own archaeology business. Her work and life were far too important to jeopardize, and she wanted to keep it that way. But then again meeting Mike wouldn't change anything if she didn't want it to.

She pulled into the Safeway parking lot, grabbed a

cart and walked into the store. OK, what do I need? She didn't have a grocery list and felt like a deer in the headlights, blinded by all her options. She started in the fruit isle which jump started her into remembering what she had come for.

Once done and on her way to the checkout she passed the liquor isle. She hesitated for a moment and then decided on two bottles of red and two of white wine. Now that she had everything she wanted, she made her way to the checkout. The lineup wasn't that bad, she only had three people in front of her. Emptying her cart, she accidentally hit the woman in front of her with a bag of salad.

"Oops, I'm sorry."

"Samantha! How are you?"

"Oh, Aloha I haven't seen you for a while." It was Chloe her neighbor.

"Aloha, yeah I've been away on Oahu for a couple of days visiting a friend of mine."

Sam edged her cart up.

"Oh, really that's nice. I haven't been for a while. How is Oahu?"

"Did you know that they tore down the International Market Place?"

"No, I didn't—that's shocking! It was a landmark."

"I know, that's just criminal."

Sam placed the last of her groceries on the conveyor belt.

"You'll never guess what they built to replace it."

"No what?" "A new improved marketplace—improved my ass. It looks just like a damn mall."

The checkout girl glanced over giving them a dirty look.

"Chloe! Watch what you're saying."

"It's true—can't they leave anything alone. We don't need new and improved just restore the original that's what I say."

"Yeah, Chloe it would be nice if they could do that, but we both know it's just a sign of progress."

Sam paid the cashier and placed her groceries in the cart.

"Well, Chloe it was nice seeing you."

"We'll have to get together soon, now that I'm back."

"For sure. Aloha."

"Aloha."

Sam wheeled her cart to the jeep and unloaded the bags. Chloe was different, but her heart was in the right place. She pulled out of the parking lot.

It wasn't long before she reached Front Street; her beach house was in sight. She pulled into the driveway, glanced at her watch. It was now five o'clock. Grabbing her backpack she walked on to the front stoop and unlocked her door.

She unloaded her groceries and carefully removed the artifacts and placed them in her desk drawer, locking it for safe keeping. Although she was running late, she uncorked a bottle of wine and poured herself a glass. She was sure that he would have left the lounge by now but perhaps there was a slim chance he was still there waiting for her. OK…OK, I'll go for old time's sake. She ran upstairs to change.

FOUR

MIKE WALKED INTO THE Tiki Lounge. He was late and wasn't sure if Samantha had come and gone. He looked around the room but didn't recognize any of the women as Samantha. The hostess greeted him, and he asked to sit facing the door so as not to miss her.

The waitress arrived with the menu and asked if he wanted anything to drink. He ordered a double shot of gin and pineapple juice. Feeling nervous, he fidgeted with the menu, opening and closing it. Doubts began to fill his mind. What if she wasn't excited to see him again, and what if she only pretended to be pleasant and then tell him to get lost? What if she just doesn't show up?

His nerves where getting the best of him. Perhaps he might have missed her as it was now five forty-five. He took a deep breath and stared at the door. Please come, he thought, taking another sip. In walked a woman who looked familiar, but was it Samantha? She looked over at him and smiled. Yes, he thought, she's here and looks more beautiful than he remembered.

He stood up as she approached his table.

"Hi, Samantha?"

"Yes, hi Mike. It's me."

"Please sit down."

Sam sat down.

"I didn't think you were coming."

"To be honest, I wasn't sure if I wanted to."

"Oh, why is that?"

"Well, first of all I was late in coming home from work and didn't think you would be here, and secondly I kept asking myself why this visit after fifteen years."

Sam could see that Mike was disappointed, but she was being honest.

"I'm glad that you did come. Yes, it has been a long time."

Mike was interrupted as the waitress handed Sam a menu.

"Sorry, but can I get you something to drink"?

"I'll have a rum punch."

"And you?" looking at Mike.

"Another gin and pineapple."

"Mahalo," said Sam to the waitress as she walked away.

"Well you look great! I must say that you are more beautiful now than when I first met you."

Sam blushed; she wasn't used to complements.

"Thank you and you—you haven't changed much."

The waitress returned with their drinks.

"Oh, yeah, you're just being kind. I'm sure I have, but thank you anyway."

"No, really you haven't." She smiled.

Mike picked up his glass. "Shall we toast to the good old times?"

Sam picked up her glass. "All right, to the good old times."

"So, tell me why after fifteen years?"

"Well for one thing it's not cheap to fly over here, and honestly I wasn't sure you would want to see me again."

"What made you take the initiative?"

"I just couldn't get you out of my mind. Oh, believe me I've tried to forget about you, and unfortunately in doing so I made a few bad choices."

Sam lowered her glass. "Well I must admit I thought about you too."

"You have?" Mike was surprised.

"What are you smiling at? Yes, I really have thought about you!"

"Good thoughts, I hope?"

"Some good, some bad."

"Fair enough. I wasn't always the best boyfriend—forgetting to buy you flowers on your birthday."

Sam smiled. "Yeah I remember that. We had a big argument over that."

"Well, I learned my lesson."

"You did at that, buying me a rose every single day."

"Yeah that I did. Let's toast to that."

They raised their glasses.

"So, what have you been up to?"

"Well, where should I start?"

"How about at the beginning," said Sam smiling.

"OK, well after you dropped me like a hot potato—"

"Hey, wait a minute, I didn't."

"Yeah, well what would you call it?"

"Things were just not working out."

"Really I thought we were just doing great."

"Is that what you thought?"

"Well, yeah." Sam leaned into Mike.

"OK, maybe we were having problems."

"Thank you," said Sam taking a drink.

"Well, after you left to travel around the world, I stayed in Napa and found work at a local dig."

"So, you did find work?"

"Yes, I did. You sound surprised."

"I thought that you weren't interested in archeology."

"I was. I just didn't make the honor roll like you did—got a bare pass."

"That's good. At least you finished the program. I know you weren't sure about the whole archaeology thing."

"It really wasn't what I thought it would be."

"Why then didn't you just get a transfer?"

"Because I wanted to be close to you to be able to have discussions on a mutual topic."Mike reached out for Sam's hand, but Sam pulled away.

"We were already dating you didn't have to do all that."

"I know but I was so in love with you, and I didn't want to lose you and in taking the course it was somewhat of a guarantee that we would always have something to talk about. And not to mention that I was with you more often."

"You're crazy."

"I know—crazy for you. But I was very insecure; and it was obviously a trait that you didn't find appealing.

"So, what did you do afterwards? I mean after we broke up."

"I took a job as a construction worker and that didn't last too long. And as far as relationships go, it took me a long time to get into another one, but eventually I did."

Sam was curious "Oh, you did? With whom?" Sam wasn't sure why she even wanted to know.

"You'll never guess?" Mike smiled.

"Do I know her?"

"Yes, you do."

"I have no idea. Give me a hint."

"OK, I'll give you a hint." Mike elevated his voice to a nasal squeal, and said Samantha really you will?"

"Oh, my gosh, her? Francis? Really?"

"Yup, you got it."

"But how and for goodness sake why?"

"Well, I was out at a club one night and she happened to be there. We danced, and one thing lead to another."

"Oh, really you got to be kidding!"

"We were both lonely and things just happened."

"How long did that last?"

"Not long. Well, you can image—after a while she just drove me nuts."

Sam took a sip of her drink almost spitting it out. "Don't make me laugh. Wow! I'm shocked."

"After you left, I was so upset and obviously not thinking right."

"Obviously, it seems so."

"After Francis I felt I was better off alone." Mike took a drink.

"Sam laughed. "I don't blame you for wanting to be alone—she could be damaging."

"Now, now be nice," said Mike, laughing.

"So, Mike, tell me why now after fifteen years have you decided to contact me?"

"Well, as I said I couldn't get you out of my mind and I wanted to see if we could rekindle what we had. Sam you and I were great together. You are the best thing that had ever happened to me."

He caressed her hand.

"Mike so much has changed. What we had was in the past and now we have separate lives. If anything we can be friends."

Mike removed his hand. "Well if that's all we can

ever be, then we'll be friends. If that's your final decision, then friends we are. I just couldn't bare not having you in my life at all."

Sam smiled and patted his arm. "Good I'm glad that you agree."

Mike smiled, grabbing his drink and looking over the rim of his glass. "We'll start at that and see what happens."

"Oh you!" Sam slapped his arm and laughed.

"OK. Now I really need something to eat," said Mike. "I'm feeling these drinks."

"You know, you're right they kind of sneak up on you." Sam opened her menu. "So how long will you be in Maui?"

Mike spotted an item on the menu that seemed appealing "Well that's what I also wanted to talk to you about."

"What's that?" Sam glanced up from her menu.

"Since you have your own company and I'm not working would you be able to hire a bare pass archaeology student?"

Sam continued looking at the menu even though she knew what she was ordering.

"You know I'm curious how did you know I had my own business?"

"Well, it stands to reason that an honor student who loves her profession would take that route."

"Hmm, hats off to you Sherlock—you're absolutely right."

"Why, thank you Watson."

"But actually, I really don't need anyone right now."

Sam placed her menu on the table.

"Oh, I see. Fine, then are you ready to order?"

Mike looked away, looking for the waitress.

Sam knew he was upset. "Mike, Mike."

"Yeah what? Don't worry about it. I understand."

"Oh Mike. OK then we'll give it a try, but you do understand that it will be strictly professional. You will not be given any special privileges, and you will do what I ask without question. Do you understand?"

Mike jumped up and wrapped his arms around her shoulders. "Absolutely! You're the boss."

"Yeah, and don't you forget it because the minute you do, friends or not, you're out."

"For Sure!"

"Then good—you start tomorrow."

"Thank you! Thank you!"

"Hey, that's Mahalo. You're in Hawaii, remember?"

"Oh right, sorry Boss, Mahalo." Mike laughed and returned to his seat.

"Now let's have something to eat, we have an early start in the morning."

Mike raised his hand for the waitress.

"What are you having, Sam?"

"Hmm, everything looks so good. I think I'll have a shrimp lettuce wrap, and you?"

"I'll have your house burger with fries," Mike said to the waitress.

"I have dibs on your fries," Sam said.

"OK, you're the boss."

Mike and Sam handed the waitress their menus.

"So, Mike how did you know I was in Maui?"

"I have my sources."

"No really, how did you know?"

"Well, in college all you would talk about is how much you loved Hawaii, Maui specifically, so I just put two and two together."

"I guess I did talk your ear off about this gorgeous place."

The waitress returned with their food.

"This looks really good." Mike was quick to take a bite of his burger not realizing how hungry he really was.

Sam reached on to his plate to steal a fry.

"Yes, really good, I've forgotten how good the food is here—it's been awhile."

"It looks like a popular place; it's getting busy now." commented Mike, taking a drink.

"It sure is. Oh look, we're about to be serenaded."

Sam glanced over her shoulder as a three-piece band was setting up. "That's what I love so much about the islands, pretty much everywhere you go there's beautiful music."

"That is nice. I could get used to it. Well, I'm done." Mike placed his knife and fork on to the plate.

"You ate that pretty quickly, but you're not quite done. You left a fry."

"Where?" Mike looked at his plate.

"Right there." Sam grabbed it. "Got you!"

"Yeah, you did. Wow, that was so good. I didn't realize how hungry I was."

"Me too. It definitely hit the spot. Well, ready to go?"

"Yes." Mike pulled out his wallet and paid the bill, leaving a generous tip.

"Mahalo," said Sam to the waitress as they walked out of the lounge.

"So, do you need a ride?" asked Sam, holding the door open for Mike.

"No, actually I'm closer than I thought. A few minutes that way. I could use the walk."

"Oh, that's right you're at the Days Inn, but are you sure?"

"Yes, I'm sure."

"OK, then I'll pick you up at seven thirty in the morning. Will you be ready?"

"Yes, that will be great. Sam can I give you a hug?"

Sam's body became rigid as Mike drew closer.

"Well, OK, but just this once." Sam smiled. "I wouldn't want you to make it a habit."

Mike wrapped his arms around her; she felt so warm and soft. Sam held on for a moment but then quickly pulled away as his warm cheek touched hers.

"Good night, Mike."

"Good night." She turned and walked away, stopping for a moment. She felt compelled to turn and watch him leave, but instead maintained her composure and continued her walk back to the jeep. Mike watched as she walked away. His feelings for her were once again resurfacing. Once she was out of sight he turned and walked back to the hotel.

Driving home she wasn't sure what had just transpired. For a brief moment she felt something that she hadn't felt in years and it was nice. But in all reality the past was just that the past, and sometimes past relationships were better left buried. Mike would just remain as a good friend, and that was all. After all she really didn't have many friends from the past, and perhaps it would be nice to have someone in her life that knew her well.

Mike unlocked the door of his hotel room and turned on the lights. He poured himself a night cap, took a long sip and then reached for the phone and made his call.

"Hello. It's me." He waited for a response. "It's all set"

He hung up and downed his drink.

FIVE

TOM AND WALLY WATCHED, hidden in the shadows, as Mike and the girl parted their separate ways.

"Who's the girl? Wally, have you ever seen her before?" asked Tom.

"No. I don't know who she is."

"Well, I'm sure we'll find out soon enough. They looked pretty cozy. I'm sure they'll be seeing each other again."

They walked up the street.

"Wally are you hungry?" Wally said nothing. "I know I am, and I know what I want—ribs!"

"There's a place just down this road, Daddy's Smokehouse."

"Oh yeah. Is it good?"

"Pretty good."

"Let's check it out."

Tom and his enormous Hawaiian, whose real name was Wai 'oli in Hawaiian, but since he had a hard time pronouncing it, he nicknamed him Wally. They turned a corner off the main street and entered a green building. The hostess immediately showed them to their table. Wally and Tom placed their orders; he could feel his mouth salivating in anticipation.

Tom was from the mainland, Texas originally. He had met Mike in the past, but on this occasion it was at the MGM Grand Casino in Las Vegas. Mike was on a winning streak and like so many gamblers turned cocky and lost his shirt. Luckily for Mike, Tom was watching him play out his winning fantasy.

As Mike was leaving the table, Tom approached him with a proposition to lend him money, so that he could continue playing. Once again Mike placed his converted chips on the roulette table, hoping for a red eight, only to lose once again. Tom took Mike aside and demanded payment.

Knowing that Mike was incapable of repaying he gave him a designated time to recover his losses. Mike agreed. Tom made a very rewarding living on scamming the naive tourist population, rich with the false idealism of leaving Las Vegas as millionaires. Once bitten with the gambling bug the desperation would set in and they would do anything to obtain funds from anyone. Tom took great pride in knowing the precise moment to strike.

Tom gave Mike his standard one week to come up with the funds, plus a hefty interest charge. Once the week ended, he paid Mike a visit and to no surprise he had disappeared. Now the fun would begin, he loved the chase; it made the game interesting.

After exhausting his suspicions that Mike remained in the vicinity of Las Vegas, he made inquiries at the airport. As predicted, Mike was leaving the country and boarding a flight to Hawaii Maui. Tom had never been to Hawaii and was looking forward to continuing his chase in paradise. After all it could also prove to be therapeutic as well as work. Once he landed in Maui, a local source connected him with the muscle he needed to intimidate Mike.

The waitress returned with their meals. Wally had ordered the same.

"Eat up my friend," said Tom, tucking the napkin under his collar, "Tomorrow we have a full day."

Wally nodded; he made a choice long ago to say as little as possible when it came to work. His opinions where best kept to himself. Although he didn't say much he was not to be underestimated, his intelligence far surpassed any of the men that had hired him.

Wai ʻoli was a full-blooded Hawaiian and was very proud of his heritage. Married with four children, two boys and two girls. He hated his job, but it paid well, more than any of the touristy jobs.

Hawaii was an expensive place to live for any single person let alone having a wife and four children, which made it all the more difficult. He did try working in the tourist industry but found that he was continually aggravated by the Haole's (Caucasians). Not all Haole's disrespected the Hawaiian culture, but unfortunately the ones he had come in contact with did.

Through some mutual friends he found that assisting the mainland thugs as muscle, he was paid well and could support his family. He didn't want to commit any crimes on the island, and that being said he would slowly disappear if the muscle would suddenly change to becoming an assassin.

He had never killed anyone and was not about to start for anyone or for any amount of money. He was only hired as a scare tactic, and he was not about to cross the line. This he kept to himself and would speak as little as possible; he had no interest in knowing them, or they knowing him.

"Wally, how do you like it?" Tom asked, his lips red with the barbeque sauce.

"Yes, it's good." Wally took another bite.

"Good. Big boy, would you like another order?"

Wally did like the perks that came with the job. "Sure."

Tom flagged the waitress.

"Yes, can I get you something?"

"Yes honey, can we have another order of ribs?"

"Just one Sir?"

"Just one for my big boy here—he needs a whole pig." Tom laughed.

The waitress looked at Wally.

"No just kidding. One order of ribs, and can I have a drink?"

"What would you like?"

"One of your fruity drinks," said Tom flashing a big smile.

"Have you ever tried a Mai Tai?"

"No." Tom moved in closer to her; he thought he was a prize catch.

"It has dark and light rum mixed with fruit juice."

"Oh, baby that sounds good. Wally want one?"

"No, I'm good. Just another water."

"I'll be right back with your orders." Tom winked at her as she walked away. Tom was under the delusion that he was a chick magnet, but in all reality, he was a short, balding little man, with an obnoxious flair when it came to communicating with women.

The waitress returned with the second order of ribs and placed the drink in front of Tom, careful not to make any eye contact.

"Thank you," said Tom eyeing her backside.

Wally disgusted with Tom's actions turned away, thinking, what a fool. Once they had finished their meal, Tom paid the bill, leaving the waitress a rather large tip along with a flirtatious gesture. He would revisit the restaurant again; the food was more than satisfactory and so was the waitress.

"So Wally, do you want to go for a drink?" Tom asked as they walked on to the main street.

"No, what time to you want me in the morning?"

"Six thirty. I want to get an early start."

"OK. I will meet you where?"

"Across the street from my hotel. I rented a car, it's

a dark grey Chevy Cruze. I'll be waiting for you.

Wally nodded in agreement then turned and walked away in the opposite direction.

Tom stood in the middle of the street watching as Wally walked away until he was no longer in sight. What a nut, he thought. Tourists were still swarming the streets even though it was late. A group of young girls walked past him, giggling and talking loudly among themselves. Tom yelled at them, trying to include himself in their conversation. He was quickly ignored but persisted by walking beside them. With all the scantily clad girls, he was loving Hawaii more and more.

"So tell me, where are you beautiful girls from?"

SIX

S AM'S ALARM RANG, AND she rolled over hitting the snooze button. She could use the extra ten minutes. Her eyes still closed, she replayed her dream, which was the same reoccurring dream. This time there was something different, she thought hard, what was it?

The images replayed in her mind, pausing at an image she did not recognize. Far off in the distance there was a ship anchored in a bay. The ship was what looked like a military ship, abandoned and rusted. Now her dream was becoming more confusing and all the more difficult to decipher.

The alarm sounded its annoying reveille, snapping her back into reality. She rolled over hitting it with her hand and shut it off. Sam stretched her long lean body, pulled the covers off and dangled her legs over the edge of the bed searching for her slippers. She had slept in and would have to miss her daily routine. Now that she was up, coffee was the first priority followed by a shower.

Once dressed it was into the kitchen to fill her backpack with snacks and bottles of ice water which she had placed into the freezer the night before. She found as the day progressed the ice would slowly melt, and her water would remain cold, which was refreshing on a hot day. It was a little tip she had learned from one of her co-workers.

Sam wondered if Mike was awake as she turned the ignition of her jeep into life. Just as she was backing up a large pit bull came running out of nowhere and barricaded her in her driveway. Oh, just great! She was late as it was. She shook her hands in the air and yelled, but the dog only moved an inch.

Frustrated, she laid on the horn. The sound scared him into action, and he ran across the road. Finally, she could continue to back up. Funny, she had never seen the dog before, maybe they purchased a new dog or it belonged to the neighbor's son, who must have been visiting.

Once on the highway, the traffic was quite light and flowed smoothly. She switched on the radio and searched for the local channel KPOA. She thought about how blessed she was to be able to live in such a lovely place.

The islands were her true love. She never could understand why battles were fought over the rites to dominate a land, until now. Yes, conquering land was a symbol of power, but she felt in the case of Hawaii it was more than that to her. The land called to her, beckoning her to come home. A feeling that was so strong she couldn't find anything comparable, except perhaps the deep love between a mother and child.

She looked into her rear view mirror and smiled. Hawaii was her one and only love, and if a man did come into her life, he would always be second. She was now in Kehei; the streets were occupied with hungry tourists. Undoubtedly, looking for a good place to have breakfast. Nearing the Days Inn hotel, she could see Mike at the entrance ready and waiting.

"Morning," Mike said, handing her a coffee.

"Morning, thank you. What's this?" Sam reached for the Styrofoam cup.

"I thought you might like a little Kona coffee."

Mike climbed into the jeep.

"How did you know?" Sam smiled.

"Just a wild guess that it might be your favorite blend."

"Why, thank you kind sir."

She took a sip and placed it in the side console. "Well are you ready?"

Mike held his backpack in his lap. "As ready as I'll ever be. What do you think of my pack? I picked it up at the ABC last night."

"Well, it's certainly quite colorful!"

"Yeah, I thought the flowers were a good touch."

"Put it this way, you'll definitely stand out." Sam smiled.

Mike laughed. "I'll have to guard it with my life because I'm sure everyone will want it."

"Oh, I'm sure they will. "Here, throw your pack in the back seat."

Mike aimed for the center of the seat. Bullseye. He then took a sip of his coffee.

"So where are we going?"

"Have you ever heard of the Iao Valley?"

"Hmm, no—"

"It's a beautiful area which is rich in history. How about King Kamehameha?"

"Yes, I have."

"Then you know that King Kamehameha won a great battle in the valley and in doing so unified all of the Hawaiian Islands. So, as you can image, the area is rich in artifacts."

"This sounds exciting! I can't wait to see it."

"Oh, you'll be doing more than just site seeing."

"Oh, oh. I hear the voice of authority."

"You do, do you? Well good," smiled Sam.

Mike lightly slapped her leg.

"Hey, come on, show a little respect here—remember who's in charge." Sam glanced at Mike.

"Somehow I don't think you'll let me forget that." Mike smiled.

"Drink your coffee!" ordered Sam.

"Yes Boss."

Sam turned the volume louder on the radio. A song came on that she liked. They sat in silence, listening to the soothing music.

Sam peered into her rear view mirror and noticed a dark grey vehicle that seemed to be following them. She wasn't quite sure if it was her imagination, but she could have sworn that they had been following her since she picked up Mike. She was careful not to lose sight of them.

Tom decided to keep his distance when he had noticed her checking the rearview mirror. He decided to ease off.

"Where do you think they're going?" asked Tom.

"Don't know." replied Wally.

"No idea? Come on you must know."

"Nope, none," said Wally looking straight ahead.

"Well, I guess we'll find out."

Tom turned left and followed them on to the highway.

"What a gorgeous day! Look the palms are swaying to the music." Sam swayed back and forth following them.

"You know, you're right they are moving in perfect unison. Look, there are people out on the beach. This early?"

"Once the sun rises, there's no other place to be."

"They're really set up with their picnic baskets and tents."

Mike turned towards Sam "I know I shouldn't ask, but can we do that?"

"What?"

"Pack a picnic lunch and spend a day at the beach? Can we?"

Sam glanced over at Mike, who was raising his eyebrows and making them dance followed with a silly smirk. Sam smiled and continued her gaze on the road.

"Come on please, please," begged Mike.

Sam exhaled. "OK, we will."

Mike was acting like an excited silly little child, reminiscence of days that were long gone—their youth. He had always found humor in everything; it seemed this was his greatest achievement, making her laugh. It was nice that part of him hadn't changed.

"So, when can we go? What should we get?" Mike asked, tapping the dash with his fingers.

"Hold on Mister. You're acting like a child. Let's get through this day before we make any plans."

Mike stopped tapping. "All right. Fine."

They were now gaining elevation, getting close to the valley. Sam thought of work and what duties she would give Mike, something relatively easy at first.

Tom remained out of sight, parked at the side of the road. From where he sat their vehicle was in clear view. He watched as they descended down the slope and around the corner.

"Now do you know where they're going?" He glanced over at Wally.

"Yes, I believe that we are now in the Iao Valley." Wally remained expressionless, eyes fixed on the road.

"Really? I'm amazed you knew that," smirked Tom "I wonder why they're here—a little sightseeing maybe?"

"Maybe," said Wally.

They watched as the jeep made several turns and ended up in a large parking lot. Once the jeep had parked, Tom eased the car forward, only to come to a full stop when he noticed they were now exiting the jeep.

Tom squinted his eyes from the blinding sun, trying to get a clear view of the woman. She was someone he had never seen before. He watched as the two wandered off on to a path that was hidden by trees.

"Come on. Let's go." Tom eased the car into a parking stall. Stepping out of the car Tom adjusted his shorts, which had rolled up on him into an area that was not comfortable.

Wally turned in time to see the adjustment and quickly looked the other way, whispering to himself, idiot Haole. Once Tom was comfortable, the stalking continued.

"This is such a beautiful place." Mike had never seen such beauty.

"It sure is and can you believe it, this is our worksite."

"Whoa! Nice!"

"Being an archaeologist does have its perks—here have some water."

Sam handed him a bottle of ice water. "You do have to watch it, you can get dehydrated quite quickly."

Mike drank some of the ice cold liquid and handed it back to Sam.

"No you can keep that one. I have several."

"OK. Thanks." He placed it in his pack.

The path that was well protected from the sun's

rays by the overhanging canopy of trees was now exposed to the direct intense sun.

"Look at the crowd of people here," said Mike. "I thought since it was so early that no one would be here."

"No. Some people like to get out very early in the morning before it gets too hot."

"I can see that." Mike wiped his forehead under his cap.

They walked on to the site, careful not to trip over any of the surveyor's tape that was carefully place around each dig.

"Come, I'll introduce you to the people you'll be working with."

Mike had noticed that he was being watched by several young men who were curious as to who he was. They lifted their heads as he walked by. Mike gave them a nod and quickened his pace to catch up to Sam.

"This is Lani. She is my foreman, so to speak," explained Sam.

"Hello. Nice to meet you." Mike smiled.

"Nice to meet you too," said Lani.

"Lani, Mike and I are old friends. We went to school together."

"Oh, that's nice." Lani looked over at Mike.

"It was a long time ago; he's also an archaeologist but hasn't been on a site in years. So, he might need a bit of a refresher."

"Oh, I see. No problem I'll help him if he has any questions," said Lani, smiling.

"Mahalo Lani. So, if you can help set him up and perhaps give him a run through of what you've been working on."

"OK, I will. Mike if you want to follow me?"

Mike looked at Sam for conformation.

"Mike, go on. See what you can remember from school. I'll check on you in a bit." "Sure." Mike followed Lani.

"Nice backpack."

"You like it, hey?"

"Nice!"

"I'm glad you do." Mike smiled.

Tom and Wally watched, hidden from sight by a large shrub. "What is this?" asked Tom.

"It's an archaeological dig," replied Wally.

"Oh, interesting. It looks like she could be—what do you call it?"

"Archaeologist," said Wally expressionless.

"Hmm, I wonder what Mike has to do with all this?" Something rustled in the brush, which made Tom jump. "What the?" A bird ran past them. "Damn bird."

Tom returned to his crouching position.

"Maybe she just wanted to show him what she did for a living," said Wally.

"Yeah, but something tells me there's more to it than that."

Tom wiped his forehead. "Man, it's hot. I need water."

He stood up. "Let's go; it looks like they'll be here

for a while."

They retreated into the coolness of the canapé.

"Hey Wally, we have to find out the connection between the two of them."

"Oh, I'm sure we will," said Wally.

Lani gave Mike a rundown about the importance of the site. Then she supplied him with tools and walked him to an area that had been sectioned off.

"This is where I've been digging, so if you like you can start here." said Lani.

"Sure, this looks like a good place to start."

"So, I'll just leave you then. If you have any questions, I'll be right over there," she said pointing to another location.

"OK, sounds good. Mahalo Lani."

Mike lowered himself into a small pit about 3 feet deep by 3 feet wide. He found a brush that Lani had obviously used and started to brush away the rich red soil. He envisioned his college professor pointing his long boney fingers at him telling him where to dig and what he should be looking for.

He was amazed at how the lessons he had learned in class were still deeply ingrained in his mind. Actually, he was enjoying himself, and-time seemed to fly by. He decided to take a bit of a break and stood up searching for Sam's whereabouts.

He finally spotted her; she was talking to a huge Hawaiian man. Sam just happened to look in Mike's direction, and noticed Mike watching her.

"There's someone I would like you to meet, Makani." They walked in Mike's direction.

"Well, so this is where Lani put you," said Sam.

"Yeah, nice girl. It's amazing how easily everything I've learned just came rushing back."

"Well, that's good. She did explain to you that we are working on an ancient burial site, right?"

"Yes, she did, and the protocol involved once we did find something."

"Good job. Mike I would like you to meet Makani. He is a Hawaiian Elder."

Mike jumped out of the pit, removed his glove and extended his hand. "I'm pleased to meet you."

Makani stood in silence gazing into Mike's eyes searching for signs of his true intentions.

Mike was feeling uncomfortable and was relieved when Sam intervened by touching Makani's arm.

"Sam mentioned that you were childhood friends," said Makani.

"Well yes, a little more than friends. Let me tell you how we met."

"Mike," Sam interrupted, "Makani doesn't need to hear our story."

Mike smiled and nodded in agreement. He knew her look all too well, and it meant trouble. Best to keep his mouth shut.

"Well if we're done with the formalities Sam, I would like to discuss our find," said Makani, looking at Mike. "In private."

"OK. Mike carry on."

Mike stood by the pit watching them walk away, and then lowered himself back down.

"What was that all about?" Sam asked.

"What was what all about?"

"You know the long stare you gave Mike. You don't like him, do you?"

Makani looked over his shoulder to make sure they were far enough away from Mike.

"Sam you know how much I care about you, right?"

"Yes, I do. We are family."

"Absolutely. I just don't trust him," said Makani.

"What! What do you mean you don't? You just meet him!"

"I know and you know how first impressions of a person speak the truth to me. And the truth about Mike is that I don't trust him."

"Well—I'm speechless. I so wanted you to like him. I've known him for such a long time."

"How long has it been since you last saw him?" asked Makani.

"I don't know, about fifteen years." Sam kicked a stone away from her foot, just as a scolded child would do knowing they were wrong.

"Precisely, and in fifteen years someone that you thought you knew so well can turn out to be a totally different person."

"That is true in some cases but not in Mike's. I still

see him as being the same person I knew back then."

"Seeing him as the old and not the new?"

"Makani, you definitely have a way with words."

"I'm just trying to open your eyes; if he wanted to be in your life, he never would have stopped communication. Sometimes the past is best to leave alone."

"Oh, come on Makani, digging up the past is our specialty—it's what we do."

Makani smiled. "Yes we do, and do you know why? So that we can learn from it. So, if you feel that you need to learn something of value from this Mike, then by all means rediscover your past. But a word of advice, he is not to be trusted."

"Oh Makani, I think you're being overly protective, but if it makes you happy, OK, I will keep my eyes open."

"That would definitely make me very happy." Makani smiled. "Now back to work. How far along are you in analyzing the discovery?"

"Not far at all. I haven't started yet." Sam knew her answer would only stir up more conversation about Mike.

"Hmm, I see. A little sidetracked are you?"

"Makani, it will get done. Don't worry, regardless of Mike being in my life or not." Sam walked away smiling.

"I should hope so."

"Mike! Mike!" Mike looked up from the pit. Sam waved her hand-motioning him to come out. Mike jumped up out of the pit.

"Come on, let's go."

"What are we done for the day?" asked Mike wiping off his pants.

"For today. I have other things to do."

Sam looked at Makani.

"OK, ready whenever you are." said Mike.

"Well, Makani I'll see you in a couple of days. Come on Mike lets go."

"What you're not coming to dinner tomorrow?" asked Makani.

"Dinner? Oh yeah, that's right. Actually, no. I think I'll pass this time."

"What? No, Sam keep your date, I can find something to do," said Mike.

"No, I'm sure it would be OK with Makani if I passed—right Makani?"

"Please don't feel obligated to look after me. If you have plans, keep them."

Sam glanced at Makani for a solution. "Mike you are welcome to join us."

"Well, are you sure? If it won't be any trouble to Makani."

"No trouble at all," confirmed Makani.

"Well then I guess it's all set. What time should we be there?" asked Sam.

"See you both tomorrow at six?"

"See you then." Sam reached up and gave Makani a kiss on the cheek and whispered Mahalo.

Makani watched as they walked off site and into the thick brush.

"Don't mean to be nosy but that Hawaiian—" asked Mike.

"Makani. Yeah what about him?"

"What did he want to talk to you about?"

"Oh, it was just about an artifact that we found the other day."

"Really! What was it?"

"An old metal box and a bone."

Mike leaned into Sam. "A bone! That's strange—a bone from what? Do you know what was in the box?"

"It looked like a finger bone, but I won't know for sure until I have an analysis done. No, the box was sealed shut. I'll try and open it once I get home."

Sam unlocked her jeep.

"That's so interesting. Can I watch you?"

Mike threw his pack in the back seat.

"We'll see." Sam grabbed two bottles of water, handed one to Mike. The ice had melted and the water was warm. Hmm warm—we'll get some cold drinks once we reach town."

Sam put the jeep in reverse and headed out of the park.

Wally nudged Tom who was asleep behind the wheel. "Hey! What are you doing?" snapped Tom.

"They're leaving," said Wally

"What? Oh, OK." Tom started the car and skidded out of the parking lot.

SEVEN

"ARE YOU HUNGRY?" SAM asked, turning on to the highway.

"You know, actually I am."

"Can you reach into my pack? I brought a couple of granola bars." Mike reached into the back seat and pulled on Sam's pack, resting it on top of his lap.

"It's in the side pocket," instructed Sam.

Mike unzipped the pocket and pulled out two bars. He unwrapped one and handed it to Sam.

"Thank you. Can I drop you off at the hotel?"

"Well, I thought I was going to your house to watch you open the box."

"It would be rather boring for you. Besides I have a lot of paper work to do as well."

"Aw come on. I don't think it would be boring."

Sam looked into her rear view mirror. "Mike, really I don't think so."

"Come on, please." Mike insisted.

"No, really Mike." Sam glanced over at Mike who had his hands clasped begging for her approval.

"Well, since you're putting it that way, OK, you can."

"Great! But first can you drop me off at the hotel? I need to grab a few things."

"Sure."

Traffic was light and in no time, she was pulling into the driveway of Mike's hotel.

Mike grabbed his pack "I'll be right back."

Sam watched as Mike ran into the hotel. She turned the radio on and reclined her seat. Now for some people watching, which she loved to do.

Mike had a quick shower and dressed into some fresh clothes along with cologne. Grabbing his keys from the side table, he looked around the room so as not to forget anything. There was one thing that he had to do—his phone call.

"Hello. It's me. Yes, I found her. I am working with her—Yup. I'll let you know in couple of days."

Mike hung up and again looked around the room; he was ready to go. As he reached for the door it suddenly flew open hitting him in the shoulder.

"YOU again! We've got to stop meeting like this!"

"Wally! Teach him a lesson," ordered Tom.

Mike doubled over holding on to his stomach and tried to catch his breath.

"Stop being a smart ass or Wally will do it again. So—where do you think you're going?"

Tom and Wally pushed Mike aside as they entered the room.

"I was just on my way out," gasped Mike, trying to compose himself.

"Oh? Do you have a date?" Tom asked.

"Me no, no date."

"Come on Mike, who are you trying to kid? I've seen you with that pretty little brunette."

"Brunette? What brunette? I don't know who you're talking about."

Wally reached for Mike's arm.

"OK. Back off—she's just an old friend."

Tom paced the room and then stopped to look out of the window.

"Now that's better. Tell me more about her."

"There's not much to tell. I've known her from college and just found out that she was living here in Maui and decided to look her up. That's all there is to it."

"Well, I hope that you haven't forgotten our little agreement?"

"You haven't given me time to forget our agreement. All you've been doing is harassing me from the get-go."

"Is that what you think I've been doing? Well, Mike, I own you and I can do anything I want." Tom punched the palm of his hand. "I mean anything!"

"All right enough! You'll get paid."

"Good I'm glad we understand each other. So, Mikey what's your girlfriend's name?"

"Why? You don't need to know. She has nothing to do with this."

"Now, be nice. I just asked you a simple question. All I want to know is her name."

Wally stepped closer to Mike and punched him in the stomach. Mike flew back against the wall and hit the floor.

"Now, I'll ask you again. What's her name?" Tom stood over Mike.

"OK—Samantha Woods!" gasped Mike.

"Now that was easy. Why do you have to be difficult? Samantha Woods that's such a pretty name for such a pretty little thing."

"Don't you touch her Tom! I'm warning you!"

"Oh, I don't think you're in any position to warn me! Now tell me what she does for a living?"

"What's that got to do with anything?" Tom turned his head towards Wally.

"All right. She's an archaeologist and I'm working for her, so I can pay you off! You scum!"

Tom burst out laughing "She better be paying you a hell of a lot. Remember Mikey in a week, and we'll be watching you. Come on, Wally. Let's go—he has a date."

Tom reached for the door. "Oh, and Mike. See you real soon!"

Mike was relieved that they had finally left. He slowly pushed himself off the floor and looked into the wall mirror for any evidence of being roughed up. Satisfied, he locked the door and headed down the stairs.

What was taking him so long? Sam glanced at the hotel entrance. The two men she had noticed previously were exiting the hotel. She slumped down in her seat as they glanced over in her direction. Once she was certain that they had passed, she sat upright and watched as they walked to their vehicle. Finally, Mike exited and walked towards her.

"Hello there." He slammed the door shut.

"What took you so long?" Sam started up the jeep and reversed on to the street.

"Sorry about that. I had a quick shower." He leaned into Sam "Here smell."

"Smell what?"

"My cologne."

"Oh, yeah that does smell nice. Now go back to your side." Sam smiled and pushed on his arm.

"I'm glad you like my cologne. I bought it with you in mind."

The tourists were everywhere, oblivious to the posted walk signs, they ran across the street at any given moment and forced vehicles to stop. Sam had to be extra cautious; their actions were unpredictable.

"So where to first?" Mike asked.

"We're going to my place. Why where did you want to go?"

"Well, I thought we could grab something to eat first."

"I have enough food at my place, so I'll just make us something."

Mike started tapping at the dash. "Oh, and do you have wine?"

"Yes, I have wine too."

"I guess we're all set then." Mike smiled.

"We are." Once she reached Front Street in Lahaina, it was a slow go. The cars came to a complete stop as several people meandered across. Sam glanced into her rear view mirror to make sure that no one had followed too closely, which would have certainly caused a rear-ender if they weren't paying attention.

She watched as another group were just about to step off of the curb. Again, checking her rear view, she looked away and then back again. She recognized the two men sitting in the vehicle behind her as the same two men that she had seen at the hotel.

"What's the matter Sam? Is something wrong?"

"No. I don't think so, but it's strange."

"What's strange?"

"I'm sure I've seen those men before in the car behind us at your hotel."

Mike glanced into the side mirror. "Are you sure?"

"Well I don't know, but it sure looks like them. It could just be a coincidence."

Mike looked back again. He knew that it wasn't a coincidence; they were being followed, and he knew by whom.

The crosswalk had finally cleared, and they started to move.

"Are we almost there?" asked Mike.

"We are once we pass the next set of lights."

Sam signaled left and waited for the lane to clear.

Then she turned into her driveway.

"Looks like they weren't following us after all." Sam watched as the car stopped at the next set of lights and then turned left.

"Oh, you're right. They are turning left." Mike wondered what they were up to.

"I guess I was wrong." Sam removed her pack from the back seat and locked the door. Mike followed Sam as they walked up the front stoop.

"This is a nice place," said Mike. "I've always loved covered porches. You can sit out here when it rains."

"I often do. I enjoy watching the people and the traffic go by."

Sam unlocked the door throwing her keys into a wicker basket for safe keeping. Mike walked in and noticing the French doors, he immediately had to see what was behind them. Swinging them open led to a lanai with a few stairs, leading down to a gorgeous garden and the beach.

"Wow! This is amazing!" exclaimed Mike.

Sam followed Mike into the garden. "Do you think so?"

"Absolutely beautiful! I could only dream of having a place like this."

"You're right about the dream; this is my little dream home."

Sam watched as Mike unlocked the garden gate and walked on to the sand. "Would you like a cold drink?"

"That would be nice. Do you happen to have a beer?"

"Actually, I do. It's our local beer. Are you OK with that?"

"Local's good."

Sam walked back into the house and pulled out a couple of beers. "Here you go and its ice cold."

"Great! Thank you." Mike took a sip. "This is really good beer. I'm impressed."

"Glad you approve. Have a seat."

"I can't get over this place—it's incredible!"

"It's not anything special, but it's home."

"You're wrong on that—it's your dream home and that is very special."

"Touché, you got me. Cheers."

"Cheers. I wouldn't mind calling this home." Mike took a sip. "Where are you going?"

"To work."

"Sit down for a second. Relax."

"In a bit. I really want to see if I can open the box; then I'll relax."

"No rest for the wicked." Mike stood up and followed Sam into the house. She pulled out a key hidden from under her lamp and unlocked the desk. Finding a pair of surgical gloves, she pulled them on her hands, and then carefully removed the box.

"Is that it? It looks so small."

"I know it's not very big, but interesting nevertheless." Sam gently scraped along the edges, loosening the lid.

"Well, that came off easily. How old do you think it is?" asked Mike.

"Not too sure. Once I have it carbon dated, then I'll be able to have an accurate date."

Sam carefully lifted the lid exposing the contents, which contained a picture and a key. She lifted the contents with a pair of tweezers and placed them on a white cloth.

"This really looks interesting!" said Mike, leaning in for a look.

"Yes, it does." Sam reached for her magnifying glass for a closer examination of the photograph.

"It's a family—father, mother and two children, a boy and girl."

"Really? Can I see?" Mike examined each of the individuals. "Interesting. I wonder who they are."

"I really don't know. Judging by their clothing, it looks like they could be from the seventies."

"The seventies? That's not that long ago."

"I know." Sam examined the key. "What's strange is the key looks older than the photograph. And it seems to be made of something other than metal."

"If not metal, then what could it be made of?"

"I don't know, but it does feel like some kind of stone."

Sam held the magnifying glass over the key. "This is amazing!"

"What's amazing?" Mike moved closer.

"There. Don't you see it? They look like symbols?"

"It does—it almost looks like hieroglyphs. Sam, I thought you were able to read hieroglyphs?"

"I can, but I've never seen anything like this. Mike you know how to read hieroglyphs. Is this familiar to you?"

"I do? No, it's not."

"We did take a class together."

"Oh really? I must have skipped that class!" Mike laughed.

"You must have—among many others."

Sam placed the key back into its box. "We certainly have a lot of questions that need answers."

"We do at that." Mike handed Sam the photograph.

"Sam wait—look at the flip side of the photo. Isn't that a map?"

"You're right, it is. This island looks so familiar. Wait a minute."

Sam walked over to the window. "I believe it's that island right there—Lanai."

Mike joined Sam, holding the photo up for comparison. "There's an X right here. I wonder where that could be on the island."

Sam took a closer look. "Here, let me compare it to a map of Lanai. I'll just place it on top of the island. Well, that's interesting the X is directly on the area called Shipwreck Beach."

"Interesting and so the mystery unravels," said

Mike replacing the map back in the box.

Sam sighed, removed her gloves and walked outside on to the lanai.

Mike followed her outside. "What's the deep sigh for?"

"Just wondered. How did the box make it all the way to Iao Valley, and then there's the fingertip."

Mike took a sip of beer and finished it off. "Good question. I'm sure we'll get all the answers."

"I hope so. Mike do you mind grabbing me another beer?"

"Sure, I'll get you one."

Sam gazed out at the land mass ahead of her. Her mind was racing trying to fit in the pieces of the puzzle.

"Here you go."

"Thanks." She took a sip and placed the bottle on the table, adjusted the cushion on the chair, and sat down.

Mike leaned his arm over the table, touching Sam's. "Well girl, I guess we'll be taking a little trip."

"We certainly will be, but since I'm not familiar with the island I would like to talk to Makani before we leave."

"Why?"

"Well, I did promise to let him know what we've found in the box and to enlighten me about any traditions or folklore specific to the island. And not to mention I do have to cancel our dinner invitation."

Mike wiped the beads of sweat from his forehead.

"Are you getting warm?"

"No, I'm comfortable."

"I guess I'm just not used to the humidity."

"It does take time to get used to. Here let me change seats, so you can have the shade."

"Thanks."

"Is that better?" asked Sam.

"Yes, much better. Thank you."

"I'll give Makani a call first thing in the morning and see if we can get together."

"Why don't you call him now?"

"I would, but today is Wednesday and he meets up with his spiritual group—he's an early riser. I'll call first thing in the morning."

"You know what's best."

"But I will call Susie—she's the lab technician. I'd like to drop the box off before we venture out to Lanai. Oh, are you getting hungry?"

"Actually, I am. Now that you mention it."

"When was the last time you had a home cooked meal?"

"I can't remember, unless you count opening a can as a home cooked meal."

"Oh, no that doesn't count." Sam smiled. "Does it even count as a meal?"

"In my books yes, but not a very good one." Mike laughed. "Here do you need any help?"

"Oh no, I'm good. Just sit back and prepare yourself for the best meal you've ever had."

"OK. I'm intrigued. Are you sure you don't need some help?"

"I'm sure. Back in bit; it won't take long."

"All right. I'll just sit here and enjoy the sunset."

Sam walked into the kitchen and grabbed her phone and dialed. It rang several times, and she was just about ready to hang up.

"Hello?"

"Hi Susie; its Sam."

"Oh hi Sam. It's been awhile."

"Yes, it has. Susie I found something at a dig and would like you to have a look at it. Can I drop it off tomorrow? In the morning?"

"Sure, Sam. What is it?"

"It's a small metal box with a photo, a key and a bone."

"A bone!"

"I know it's unusual. It looks like the remains of an index finger. I just wanted you to take a look at the items."

"No problem. Where did you find it?"

"In the Iao Valley."

"Oh, are you still digging out there?"

"We are. There's lots to unearth. I should be at the lab by nine, is that all right with you?"

"Absolutely."

"Thank you, Susie. See you at nine. Have a good-night?"

"You too. See you then. Mahalo."

Mike walked down to the beach for a closer look at the sunset reflecting off the water. The spectacular colors of orange, yellow and purple blended perfectly across the crimson sky.

Although many artists have tried to capture its beauty, none could compare with nature's majestic creativity. The sun began to descend quickly into its watery horizon only to return later to lighten the morning sky. A warm breeze scented with flowers caressed his face and taking a deep breath, he inhaled the sweet fragrance.

"Mike! Mike! Dinner's ready."

Sam had the table set with two wine glasses.

"This smells and looks incredible! Here let me pour the wine." Mike opened the wine and filled the glasses. "What do you call this?"

"Lau Lau and rice."

"What is Lau Lau?" Mike picked up his fork and unraveled the greens.

"It's traditional—pork and fish wrapped in a Taro leaf then steamed."

Mike took a bite. "Hmm this is very good. I'm liking this."

Sam took a sip of wine. "Good I'm glad."

"Did you just make this?"

"Yes, I did. I made a big batch of them over the weekend to freeze for a quick meal during the week."

Mike swallowed before taking a sip of wine. "That's a great idea. So, tell me Sam why aren't you married? I mean such a beautiful and intelligent girl like you."

"Well I am married in a way to my career, but I know what you mean. I did date someone."

"Oh really, you did? I thought I was the only one."

"You were the first, so in a way you will always be the one."

"I'm flattered. I like your analogy." Mike took another bite.

"I thought you would." Sam smiled "Anyway, it took a long time—years after we had ended that I had any interest in dating again."

"Really? Well, he must have been special. What happened?" Mike took a drink of his wine.

Sam also took a drink, then placed her glass on the table. "Well, we both wanted different things. I mean he wanted to get married, but I wanted to have a career."

"Oh, similar to our situation then?"

"Yes, you could say that; he supported me, and he was always there for me in the bad times and the good times."

Mike grabbed his glass. "What happened? And where is he now?"

"Sadly, he passed away."

"Oh, I am so sorry."

"Thank you. He was a very special man. He didn't have a selfish bone in his body—he only wanted the best for me."

"Which is a rare find nowadays."

"That's for sure. We used to talk to each other every single day. Sometimes every hour of the day."

"Really? What did you talk about?"

"Different things. Great revelations; or the mundane day to day—just to hear his comforting voice."

"I can see why you would throw yourself into work. I know I would do the same."

Sam's eyes filled with tears. "It's a hard one to get over."

Mike stood up and threw his arms around her.

Sam couldn't hold back her tears. "Thank you, Mike. It's been such a long time since I've been able to talk about him."

"How long has it been, since he's passed?"

"About a year now." Sam wiped the tears from her eyes. She gave a deep sigh and reached for her wine.

"It's a difficult time for you. You're still in the grieving process."

"I know—time will heal so they say, but does it really? I don't think so. You know what I think is that you learn to cope with the loss, but you never stop hurting."

"It's very true Sam. You never stop hurting; that I know all too well."

"That's right, you would know after losing your parents."

Mike hugged Sam tightly. He could feel his eyes fill

with tears, and he quickly wiped them before she noticed.

"How did he pass away?" Mike returned to his seat.

"He had bladder cancer, they had to remove his bladder."

"Oh, Sam, I'm so sorry." Mike reached for her hand.

"He was doing fine until he developed a hernia. They operated, and he was so excited thinking that he would be able to function better once he had the operation. We had made plans once the procedure was done. He loved swimming, bike riding and our nature walks."

"What happened?"

"He got worse. He developed a massive infection and shortly afterward they found that the cancer had spread throughout his body."

"Oh Sam!"

"It wasn't long after that he was gone."

"I'm so sorry."

"You know the hardest part is that I really don't have anyone to talk to anymore, not someone who knew me as well as he did."

"Sam you know you can talk to me. I might not know you as well as he did, but I do know you."

"Thank you, Mike. You don't know how much that means to me."

Mike raised his glass. "To a lasting friendship!"

Mike refilled their glasses.

"You know Sam you were truly blessed to have had him in your life."

"Yes, I am truly very blessed."

"Sorry, but is it OK if I change the subject?" Mike asked.

Sam wiped her eyes. "Yes, please do."

"What are the plans for tomorrow?"

"Well, tomorrow we'll go see Makani and then a trip to Lanai."

"What do you think we'll find?"

"I really don't know until we're there, well hopefully…" Sam emptied her glass. "Would you like more?"

"No, I've had enough. I'm getting tired; it's been a long day."

Mike stood up "Yes it has. I'll just take a cab back to the hotel."

"You'll do no such thing. I insist that you stay."

"Well, if it's no trouble."

"No trouble at all. I'll just set up the couch."

"Couch will be fine."

Sam started to clear away the dishes.

"Here let me help you." Mike picked up the remaining dishes.

"You can just leave them in the sink. I'll deal with them in the morning. I'll just grab you a pillow and a blanket."

"Thanks." Mike walked over to the couch and removed the cushions.

"Here you go. Oh, and if you need to use the bathroom there's one just down the hall." "You have two bathrooms?"

"It's so nice—one upstairs and one downstairs."

Sam started up the stairs. "Now are you all good?"

"Perfect! That's all I need—see you in the morning."

"Night, and Mike," said Sam from the top of the stairs. "Thanks for listening."

"Anytime Sam, anytime. Night."

Sam couldn't wait to fall into bed; she was exhausted. Her crying was a contributing factor. It was nice to be able to finally release her pent up sorrow to someone whom she had a history with. She slid under the covers, laid her head on to the soft pillow and immediately fell into a sound sleep.

Mike pulled the covers over him; he was quite comfortable. He thought about Sam and what she'd been through. What a lonely life she has. Granted there were people around her but not that one person to really be there for her. No wonder she threw herself into her work. They had more in common than she would ever know. He closed his eyes and fell asleep.

"Hello. It's me, Susie."

"Hello Susie. Why are you calling?"

"I just received a request from Samantha Woods. Apparently, she found a small metal box in the Iao Valley and wants me to analyze it."

"Did she open it?"

"Yes, she did, and the contents were a picture, a human bone and a key."

"A key! How interesting. Does she know what the key unlocks?"

"No, I don't think so. She's dropping by the lab tomorrow morning."

"Thank you, Susie; keep me posted."

"Very good, will do."

Susie reached for her bedside lamp and switched it off.

EIGHT

MIKE TRIED TO ROLL over, but the blankets had somehow wrapped around him trapping him.

"Wake up sleeping beauty."

Mike opened his eyes to find himself being pinned down by Wally. Mike struggled trying to free himself.

"So, this is where your girlfriend lives," said Tom.

"What have you done to Sam?"

"Oh, that's her name. Well nothing, not yet anyways."

"If you touch her, I'll…" said Mike struggling to free himself.

"You'll what?" asked Tom looking down at Mike.

Mike said nothing.

"Yeah, that's what I thought. You know Mike, all I want is the money. Give me the money and we'll leave you alone. Plain and simple."

"Simple! Somehow I know nothing is just plain and simple with you."

"Now, now Mike. I'm a man of my word."

"Let me up!" shouted Mike.

Tom nodded to Wally who ripped the covers off Mike throwing him on to the floor. Mike felt like his body had just experienced a massive rug burn.

"Tom, I said I would give you the money. It will just take time."

"Time is what you don't have—it's up."

"Oh, come on. By the end of next week for sure."

"You know your girlfriend has a really nice place here." Tom pulled back the drapes "I like the view."

He glanced over at the desk. "What's this?" Tom flipped the lid of the metal box, exposing its contents.

Mike jumped over the couch and rushed towards the desk. "Leave that alone!"

Wally had rushed over and was now holding Mike's arms.

"It's a neat looking box. Hmm, what's inside?"

Mike struggled to free himself from Wally's grip, but his efforts were proving to be futile.

"It's nothing—just something Sam found."

"Interesting—she's an archaeologist, right? And what's this?" asked Tom holding up the picture.

"Just a picture of a family."

Tom flipped the photo around. "Now this looks very interesting—a map?"

Mike broke free from Wally and lunged forward.

"Give me that!" yelled Mike.

"Oh I don't think so." Tom held the photo out of Mike's grasp.

Wally was quick to restrain Mike before he could

reach for Tom.

"Wally where do you think this is?" said Tom turning the photo over to expose the map.

"It looks like that island out there. Lanai, and the X looks like the spot where Shipwreck beach would be."

Tom walked up to the window, and held up the map. "You know it does look like the island—the shape is very similar. Yeah, yeah, I think you're right."

"So, what's the X for? Buried treasure?"

"I don't know," snapped Mike.

"Oh, Mikey I think you know." Wally squeezed Mike's arm.

"Yeah OK—sure it's treasure. I was planning on stealing it and giving it to you to get you off of my back."

Tom circled Mike like a shark ready for the kill. He indicated to Wally to let go of him.

"Is that so? Well, you better be telling the truth. I'm a reasonable man, and I'll give you a little more time. I've never been accused of not being a fair man."

"You know whatever we find will be far more valuable than the mere fifty thousand I owe you."

"Mike, Mike with the extended time and the interest, I'm sure the treasure would be worth a whole lot more, but just so you understand I want the treasure and one hundred thousand."

"What! A hundred thousand and the treasure! Are you crazy? I only owe you fifty and if there's treasure it would be priceless. You call yourself a fair man; that's a lot of crap! You're a greedy dirty—"

"Hey! Greedy, no. This has nothing to do with greed; it's what you owe! One hundred thousand dollars and treasure—end of conversation."

"What if there is no treasure?"

"Well, for your sake there better be. Either way, one hundred thousand that's what you owe."

"Mike! Mike! Who are you talking to?" Sam stood at the top of the stairs.

Tom turned towards Sam.

"Sam Run!" yelled Mike.

Mike punched Tom in the jaw sending him to the ground, then grabbed a chair and hurled it at Wally hitting him in the head and knocking him against the wall. Mike jumped over the men, and seized the metal box. He rushed over to Sam and grabbed her hand.

"Come on let's go!"

"Who are these guys?"

"Never mind get your keys; let's get out of here. Now!" Wally was coming to.

They ran to the jeep and jumped in. Sam turned the ignition and slammed it into reverse and backed on to the street. The two men had recovered and were now standing at the doorway watching as the jeep disappeared into the night.

"Mike did you get the box?"

Mike reached into his pocket and pulled out the box. "It's right here."

Sam glanced over. "Good. Is that what they were after?"

"Well no—not really."

Sam glanced in the rear view to see if they were being followed, but it didn't look like it. "If that was not what they were after, then what?"

"Sam, I haven't been completely honest with you."

"What do you mean?"

"Well… these guys are here to collect the money I owe them. You see I have or rather had a gambling problem."

"What? Really! You were never into gambling."

"It wasn't when we were dating, but soon after I got into it."

"I hope you're not blaming me for your bad choices."

"No! Oh my goodness, no—it's totally my fault; you had nothing to do with it. It started out innocent enough—just a few bets here and there. Then it started to get out of hand, until finally it turned into an addiction. I just couldn't stop."

"Mike, how stupid!"

"I know that now, but at the time it felt like the right thing to do."

"So how much do you owe them?"

"It was fifty thousand."

"Was?"

"Yeah, unfortunately until they noticed the box and the map. Now they think there's some long-lost treasure worth millions, which of course they want."

"What! That's crazy! There's no guarantee that

we'll find anything, let alone treasure."

"I know, but regardless my fifty thousand has now turned into one hundred thousand. And I have a funny feeling if there's no treasure, I'll owe them more."

"You can't come up with that kind of money, can you?"

"Hell, no, but I'll have to find some way to get them off my back. Now hypothetically speaking if there were treasure, would we be able to keep it?"

"Absolutely not! It would belong to Hawaii."

"OK, so now that's established, I'll have to find another way to get rid of them."

Mike looked at the side mirror to make sure they weren't being followed.

"You better because I want no part of this."

"Unfortunately, my dear, you are a part of this now."

"Yeah, thanks to you." Sam reached for her water bottle.

"Here let me get it."

"No! I've got it—you've helped enough."

Mike leaned up against the door. "Look, I'm so sorry that I got you into this. Don't worry, I'll figure something out. I'll try to convince them to leave you alone."

"Damn it Mike, do you really think they'll listen? You are so naive; you really haven't changed. I'm involved now and that's that!"

Mike leaned towards Sam reaching for her arm "I'm so sorry."

"Don't! Just don't talk to me right now!"

Mike backed away. "Well can I ask you one thing?

"What?" cried Sam.

"Where are we going?"

"We're catching the first ferry to Lanai. It leaves in a couple of hours. And I need to call Makani."

"Oh, why are you calling him?"

Sam turned off of the highway and on to a dirt road that was well hidden by tall sugar canes. Once she was secure in knowing that no one could spot them from the highway she parked.

"Look I need to call Makani—he needs to know what's happened."

Mike leaned his back up against the jeep door. "Really—so you are going to tell him exactly what happened?"

"Yes! He needs to know in case something bad happens."

"Stop it! Nothing bad will happen to you. I'll protect you, or do you feel that I'm incapable?"

"I never said that."

"No, but that's what you're implying."

"Look I'm not arguing with you."

"Who is this Makani to you anyways? Are you interested in him?"

"Stop it! You're being ridiculous."

"OK, it's none of my business if you are."

"You're right, it's none of your business. Just leave it alone."

"All right, I'm sorry." Mike rolled down the window. "So, where are we?"

"We're in a sugar cane field. We'll hide out here until sunrise and then make our way to the ferry. Hopefully, they won't follow us to Lanai."

"I hope they don't, but the big guy called Wally did tell Tom that the X on the map was Lanai."

"Oh, just great! Well, let's hope that we get there before they do."

Mike stretched his legs. "What time does the ferry leave?"

"The first ferry leaves at six forty-five at the Lahaina Harbor."

"What time is it now?"

Sam looked at her watch "It's five fifteen. We'll leave soon and grab a coffee somewhere."

"That sounds good to me. I really could use one." Mike reclined his seat.

"I'll give Makani a call once we're on the ferry."

"I think I'll just close my eyes for a bit," said Mike.

"Good idea. Let's try and get a little rest; we've got a long day ahead of us."

Sam reclined her seat and closed her eyes. The wispy fingers of the trade winds gently swayed the stocks of the sugar cane and soon lulled her to sleep.

"Hey, what are you doing here?" shouted a man's voice.

Sam suddenly awoke, and jumped into action. She started up the jeep and threw it into reverse. Mike's body slammed back into the seat.

Three field hands were yelling and shaking their tools at them as they sped past them. Once she reached the road, she swung the jeep into forward motion and headed on to the highway.

"Oh man, that was close!" Mike snapped his seatbelt into place. "What a way to wake up!"

"Tell me about it." Sam's heart was pounding. "What time is it anyway?"

Mike looked over at the dash. "It's 6:05."

"We should be able to just make the ferry; it's only 20 minutes away." Sam stepped on the gas, travelling well over the speed limit.

"Sam slow down; we don't want a ticket."

"I just want to make sure we catch the ferry. Watch for cops."

The ferry was in sight, they were already loading. Sam signaled and turned right into a parking lot.

"What? Can't we take the jeep?"

"No, it's on foot." Sam found a parking spot.

"Come on, let's go! Hurry!" They ran towards the harbor, just in time to see the ferry worker welcoming one of the last tourists on board.

"You just made!" said a tourist.

"Yeah, just." Sam laughed.

They walked on board and found two seats at the back of the boat.

"Ah! We made it," sighed Sam, placing her pack down beside her. "I really didn't think we would."

Mike pulled out a bottle of water. "Do you want a drink?"

"Sure. You know what I can really use is a large coffee," Sam said, taking a long drink.

"I agree that's a priority once we get to Lanai."

Sam watched as several tourists were talking among themselves. One, a rather large obnoxious man, who obviously had a liquid breakfast was relaying a story to his group when he stumbled and fell on to the deck. The group let out a burst of laughter. A couple of the group members stood up and came to his aid, lifting him on to his seat. Sam looked past the crowd and noticed two men.

"Shit!" Sam slouched down in her seat.

"What? What is it?" Mike looked around the crowd confused by her sudden paranoia.

"Get down!" Sam pulled on Mike's arm, pinching it.

"It looks like someone else just caught the ferry."

"No way!" said Mike rubbing his arm.

"Yup."

"What are we going to do now?"

"Let's just sit here. Hopefully, they won't spot us, and if they do I really don't think they would do anything with all these people around."

Sam reached for her cell phone.

"I think you're right. They won't want to make a scene. What are you doing?"

"Calling Makani, I'm sure he's up."

"Makani, morning. It's Sam."

"Morning Sam. Where are you calling from? It sounds windy."

"I'm on the ferry—on my way to Lanai."

"Lanai! But why?"

"Well long story. I managed to open the box and found several things."

"You did! What?"

"A photograph of a family and a key."

"Really…that's interesting."

"Yes, it is interesting, but what's more interesting is that the photograph has a map drawn on the back of it."

"And you obviously recognized it as being Lanai?"

"Yes, and there was an X placed on top of an area we know as Shipwreck Beach."

"That's intriguing. Any idea why that area would be marked?"

"No. We're on our way there to see what we can find."

"So, you're not alone, I take it?"

"No, Mike is with me."

"Sam, I told you—"

"I know. I know." Sam paused ambivalent about mentioning her true reason for her call.

"Sam are you there?" asked Makani.

"Yes, I am. Makani, you're really not going to like what I have to say next."

"Go on."

"Mike got into some trouble on the mainland."

"I knew it!"

"But wait, that's just the half of it. There are two men after us. Mike owes them money from a gambling debt."

"Sam what did I tell you? I had a bad feeling about him; he can't be trusted. Just get rid of him."

"Well, it's not that easy. They broke into my house."

"Are you OK?"

"Yes, fine. They saw the map and the photograph, and now they think that the X marks a hidden treasure. They have demanded the treasure along with the money Mike owes."

"Lolo!"

"What was that?"

"Crazy! Lolo! Do you really believe that there's treasure?"

"I really don't know what we'll find."

"OK, Sam how can I help?"

"There's nothing you can really do. I just wanted to let you know—just in case."

"Sam this sounds ominous; tell you what I can do. I have some friends on Lanai; I'll call them and see if they would be able to help, maybe by scaring them off."

"Oh, would you? Makani that would be a big help."

"Leave it up to me. Now go and I'll call you back."

"Mahalo Makani, Mahalo."

"I didn't mean to eavesdrop but that sounded promising," said Mike.

"It was. Makani mentioned that he has friends on Lanai, and he would give them a call. They might be able to keep them off our backs for a while."

"For a while maybe, but then what happens once they catch up with us?"

"We'll just have to cross that bridge when we get to it, right?"

Mike grabbed his water bottle. "Right."

Sam looked over at the passengers who were sitting in front of her.

"Do you see them anywhere? I don't see them."

"No, me neither."

"I wonder where they are. Maybe best case scenario they fell overboard."

"That would be great!" Mike laughed. "Problem solved."

NINE

THE FERRY DOCKED AND the tourists were the first to eagerly disembark.

"Mike push your way into the crowd, so they can't see us."

Mike accidently pushed an elderly woman a little too hard.

"Oh, I'm so sorry!"

She said nothing but if looks could kill, he would surely have been a goner.

"Sam, there's nothing on this island, I'm so use to large hotels along the shoreline."

"It's definitely not the same as the other islands."

"Mind you, it's how I've always pictured Hawaii."

"Well, it is definitely the old Hawaii."

"Do we rent a car?" asked Mike.

"We'll need to rent a 4x4. The terrain is pretty rough."

"How do you know that?"

"I overheard one of the passengers mention it."

"Where do we go to rent one?"

"I'm not too sure, but it looks like everyone is migrating in that direction," said Sam. "I'll just confirm with someone."

Sam turned to ask, and then quickly walked back and grabbed Mike's arm.

"Come on, let's keep walking."

"Hey you!" yelled Tom.

"Mike. Run!"

"Is it them?"

"They're right behind us—hurry!" They ran and hid in between the sea of tourists. Sam turned to see if they had eluded them only to see four Hawaiian men talking to them.

"Ah, Mike stop running."

"What? Why?"

"Look! It looks like Makani came through."

"Perfect timing. Awesome!"

"Come on, let's hurry and rent that jeep."

Tom and Wally were surrounded. What do guys want?"

"We want you to back off and leave Sam and Mike alone."

Tom started walking away "This is none of your business."

Three of the Hawaiians followed Tom, one guarded Wally who wasn't about to cause any trouble with his bothers.

"No, you're wrong, it is our business. So if you know what's good for you leave this island, and leave it now!"

Tom was being surrounded, making him very nervous.

"No! I told you. My business is with them and not you."

One of the men pushed Tom to the ground. "Well, we're making it our business and we want you to leave!"

Tom struggled to get up only to be immediately pushed back down. Wally watched as the intimidation continued.

"Back off man," shouted Tom as he struggled to get up.

"We'll back off only if you say you're leaving."

"OK! Fine, enough man. We're leaving."

"Here let me help you up." One of the Hawaiians pulled on Tom's arm sending him flying.

"It's nice to know that we understand each other."

He patted Tom on the back and looked at Wally.

"What's up Brah?" Wally asked.

"Nothing now Brah. What are you doing with this haole?"

"Brah, I need the money."

"I hope he's paying you a lot."

"Yeah Brah, you know never enough."

Tom walked back to Wally. "What are you talking about?"

"Nothing. Let's go."

"The ferry is waiting, so start walking," ordered the Hawaiian.

Tom and Wally walked to the dock and boarded

the ferry.

"Good. Now don't come back or..." yelled the Hawaiian who was hitting his fist into the palm of his hand. Tom flipped him the finger. The Hawaiians rushed up on to the dock for a little added intimidation, which worked. Tom remained hidden until he was certain they had left.

"I'm sure we scared the crap out of him. Come on let's go." Makani's men walked towards their truck.

"Hey, Brah, give me your cell phone I want to call Makani."

"Why don't you use yours Brah?"

"Just give it."

"Aw man. No. Where's yours? Let me guess... you didn't pay your bill again, yah? Aw Brah! Not again! You know that you have to pay your bills one day, right?"

"Yeah, yeah. Just give me your phone." Reluctantly he handed it to him.

"Hello Makani. We gave them a good scare. I don't think they'll be bothering anyone for a while."

"Did Sam get away?"

"They were headed towards the rental."

One of the Hawaiians glanced over towards the ship just in time to see Tom and Wally jump off.

"Wait Brah, the two of them just jumped ship."

"Great! Get them!"

"Makani, I'll call you back. Come on let's go."

The four Hawaiians ran towards the ship. Tom and Wally ran in opposite directions, ducking in and out of the crowd of tourists.

Sam and Mike jumped into their rental and sped out of the parking lot on to the dirt road.

"Look, Sam, there's four big Hawaiian dudes running after Tom and Wally."

"Sam glanced in the rear view mirror. "Good that must be Makani's men. I'm sure they'll keep them busy for a while."

Mike turned around in his seat to watch the show.

"That's for sure—look at them run! They don't know where to run, quite comical actually. Well, since they're going to be busy for a while can we get a coffee somewhere?"

"Absolutely, once we get far enough away."

"This island is so remote. I just love it. It's like going back into the past."

"It does feel that way," said Sam, "I wish all the islands would have remained the same way."

"Unfortunately, progress has other plans."

"Exactly! What bothers me are the million dollar hotels that locals can't afford to stay in. After all it is their land, and they should be entitled to the good things in life without paying an exorbitant amount."

"What would be even better," said Mike, "would be free accommodation."

"That would be ideal. And if there was a problem conflicting with their tourist season, well offer it off season. Oh, I need a coffee," said Sam, "I'm getting too deep."

"Is that a problem? But I definitely agree that Hawaiians deserve more perks."

"Look! There's a cafe just up the road," said Mike.

Sam accelerated and then pulled into the parking lot.

"Come on, let's go." Mike jumped out of the jeep.

"Hey wait up!" shouted Sam.

They walked up the stairs into an old wooden building. Mike held the door for Sam.

"This is so cute. It looks like a small beach shack," enthused Sam.

"Yes, it looks like one in the Frankie Avalon beach movies. And look they're not busy. This is great!"

"Morning, for two?" A pretty young girl asked holding two menus.

"Yes, for two," replied Mike.

The waitress showed them to their booth, which was situated by a window.

"We'd like two coffees, please," said Sam as the waitress handed her the menu.

"Frankie Avalon?" asked Sam.

"Hmm…what?"

"You said this place reminded you—"

"Oh yeah, you know the guy that lived on the beach in his little hut."

"I think you mean Gidget and Moondoggie."

"Oh, you're absolutely right. What a great movie; they don't make wholesome movies like that anymore."

Sam smiled. "No, they don't. I wonder what your

friends are doing."

"Oh, Tom and Wally. Yeah, it was funny watching them run in all directions. You know that was really nice of Makani to help us. You'll have to thank him for me."

"Yes, it was—he's such a sweetheart." Sam took a sip of her coffee

"Well, I guess it's off to Shipwreck Beach. I wonder what we'll find."

"I wonder—this should prove to be very interesting." Sam closed her menu and handed it to the waitress.

"Have you decided?" asked the waitress.

"Yes. Are you ready Sam?"

Sam nodded.

The waitress placed their order and refilled their coffees.

"Wow! We ordered a lot of food."

"Well, it's good we did because it will have to tide us over for a while," said Sam.

"I'm sure it will. Sam, I'll be right back—I need to use the washroom wherever that is."

"I think it's just down there." Sam pointed towards an alcove, which indicated the location of the washrooms.

"Oh, yeah, I see it—be right back."

Mike walked down a narrow hallway towards the men's room, when he noticed a phone that was well hidden from prying eyes. Picking up the receiver he made his call.

"Hello…Hello operator, I would like to make a long-distance call to Washington, DC."

"That will be five dollars please."

"Can you reverse the charges?"

"Yes, and what is the number and whom shall I say is calling?"

"This is Mike North and the number is—Hey buddy! Watch what you're doing! I'm on the phone here! Sorry a guy just bumped into me—did you get the number?"

"Yes, I did. One moment please while I try that number."

"Who's calling me at this hour?"

"Hello, this is the operator. Will you accept the charges from Mike North?"

"Jerry, it's me. Mike from Hawaii."

"Yes, operator. I'll accept the charges."

"Go ahead," said the operator.

"Mike, it's about time I heard from you. What's going on?"

"I'm in Lanai."

"Where?"

"Lanai—a little island off Maui. Anyway, Sam found a small metal box."

"Yes, I know all about that."

"What? How did you know?"

"Do you really think that you would be my only connection? Let's just say from a very reliable source who keeps me informed at all times."

"Then what do you need me for?"

"Exactly. I've been asking myself that question."

Mike was surprised by his comment. "Anyway, I'll just ignore that remark," said Mike, annoyed.

"Take it any way you want. Does this Samantha know anything about the artifacts?"

"No, nothing."

"If she's such an expert as my contact has mentioned, then I'm sure it will only be a matter of time before she figures it out."

"I agree with you there; she is a smart one, and I know she will in no time."

"If she does, you know what to do right?" said Jerry.

Mike took a deep breath—second guessing his involvement.

"Mike are you still there?"

"Yeah…yeah sure." He held the receiver in his hand until he heard the dial tone and then hung up.

"What took you?" asked Sam when he returned. "Your breakfast is probably cold by now."

"I'm sure it's all right." Mike looked down at his plate of food and suddenly felt his appetite fade.

"Mike are you all right?"

"I'm good." He raised his hand and the waitress returned and filled their cups with coffee.

"You're not eating—aren't you hungry?" Sam asked as she ate her breakfast.

"I just wanted more coffee first."

Sam occasionally tried to strike up a conversation, but Mike was unresponsive concentrating on his meal.

"You know if you're done, we should be going. Makani's guys won't be able to hold them off for very long."

"Done! Let's go!" Mike said, angrily pushing his plate to the side.

"No need to get defensive!" Sam grabbed her bag.

Mike stood up as the waitress was returning. "May I have the check?"

Sam reached for her wallet.

"No, I've got this."

"I insist, I'll get it."

Mike glared at her. "OK fine. Then I'll see you at the jeep."

Mike pulled out his wallet, gave the waitress the amount with a small tip. As he left the restaurant, he could see that Sam had already started the jeep. Mike reached for the door handle and was quickly thrown back as Sam threw the jeep into reverse. He held on to the swinging door, using it as a lever to jump on to the seat.

"Are you crazy? What are you doing?" yelled Mike as he managed to slam the door shut.

"What? I'm driving—what do you think I'm doing?"

Mike made the decision not to comment and just stared at the road in front of him. They drove in silence, on occasion, sharing an angry glance.

TEN

JERRY TALBOT SEARCHED FOR his slippers and placed his robe over his large body. Walking into the bathroom, he turned on the tap and splashed his face with cold water, gazing up at his reflection and examining his chiseled features. Satisfied with his image, he continued to brush his teeth. Walking back into the bedroom, he reached for the phone and made a quick call.

"Hello Andrew. Can you get the private jet ready? We're taking a little trip."

"Very good, Sir, but may I ask where?"

"To Maui in Hawaii, so pack appropriately."

"Very well, Sir. Will ring you once it's all arranged."

Jerry hung up and grabbed his suitcase and started to pack when the phone rang again. "Yes?"

Mr. Talbot the plane is ready whenever you are."

"Good. I'll be ready in forty-five minutes; you can send the car around."

"Very good, Sir."

Jerry was uncertain about what to pack, he was not accustomed to taking vacations, let alone a trip to the tropics. He finally settled on a few T-shirts and a pair of shorts. He had just finished when the phone rang again.

"Mr. Talbot your car is here," said Andrew.

"Thank you. I'll be right down."

Jerry locked his luggage, added a few folders to his briefcase, and also locked it. He took one last look around the room for any items that may have been overlooked; satisfied he attached the handcuffs to his wrist and secured his briefcase. Leaving the apartment, he picked up his luggage and locked the door behind him. The elevator doors opened, and a couple greeted him with a nod and a smile, which Jerry reciprocated.

They rode in silence listening to the elevator music. The doors opened and once again a parting smile and nod. The lobby was immaculate, adorned with large modern day statues in bronze that were stunning in contrast to the black marble flooring. Jerry had lived in the condo for thirty plus years, ever since he had been hired by Special Forces.

"Sir, the plane is ready."

Jerry handed Andrew his suitcase but held on to the briefcase.

"Thank you." Once Jerry was comfortable, Andrew assisted by shutting the limousine door.

"Sir, we should be at the airport shortly," said Andrew from the passenger seat.

"Very good."

The limousine pulled on to the deserted streets. Jerry watched as his massive apartment building faded off in the distance. It was a complete contrast from his poverty-stricken upbringing.

His family had emigrated from Ireland and made their home in New York. They didn't have much, but his parents made the best of what they had. His parents were married for twenty years, and their love was as fresh as the first time they met.

Jerry was the only child, but he was never spoiled. He had to work for his allowance and that meant getting a job as a paperboy. His father was a bartender at a local bar and his mother a seamstress. Once Jerry had returned from school his mother would be just arriving home from work.

He would often help his mother prepare dinner before his father came home for dinner. His father would many times join them for dinner on his break from the pub. One-night when dinner had been prepared and the table set, there was a knock at the door. His mother laughed and muttered that his father had forgotten his keys. She unlocked the door to see two police officers. Jerry ran to her side.

"Are you Mrs. Mary Talbot" asked one officer.

She nodded. "Yes?"

"There's been a terrible fight, and I need you to come with us to identify the body."

"No!" his mother screamed. "There must be a mistake!"

The officer insisted that she come with them.

Jerry glanced up at his mother, who was slowly losing her balance.

The officer caught her before she reached the floor and helped her on to a chair.

Jerry asked if he could go instead, and the officers agreed.

Jerry kissed his mother goodbye and suggested that she go and lie down. He helped her to her bed and assured her that he would be right back.

Jerry followed the officers out to their car. As he sat in the back seat, the reality started to flood his mind. They must have made a mistake; it couldn't be his father. He was certain that they had wrong person.

The car stopped in front of the city morgue. They walked into the dismal building and were soon ushered down a long grey hallway. Jerry was beginning to feel as automatic as the doors silently opening and closing.

They entered a room that was sterile with one table and several metal compartments on the side of a wall. A man in a white coat mentioned something to one of officers. Jerry heard nothing that was being said only witnessing words that were being carefully formed on their lips. They had motioned for him to join them, but his body had become immobile. He tried to move but his feet were firmly planted on the steel grey floor. One of the officers assisted him to a large metal compartment stacked on the wall along with many others. The man in the lab coat pulled on the handle, and an officer motioned for him to look down. Jerry reluctantly obeyed. There on a table lay a body with a sheet over it. He watched, transfixed as the sheet was carefully pulled back revealing a figure who resembled his father.

"Is this your father?" asked the officer.

Jerry wanted to yell—no, no, it's not him! It can't be him!

Jerry took another look, and sadly nodded his head confirming the fact.

Later on, they learned what had happened. His father had broken up a fight in the bar and one of the men had pulled out a knife stabbing him, repeatedly. A few of the customers ran after him as he tried to escape, and he was quickly apprehended.

Jerry leaned back looking out at the passing buildings. For years he felt that it was his father's fault— if only he had minded his own business, he would have lived to see him grow up and his mother would have still been alive today. She died shortly after from a broken heart, no doubt. Jerry was alone and ended up in a foster home. As soon as he was of age, he joined the Navy and that's when he decided that his life would be one of service.

The car pulled into the hanger. Andrew retrieved the luggage and they walked out on to the tarmac. A private plane was ready for the two men to board. Once seated the steward entered the cockpit to inform the captain that they were ready for takeoff. Jerry buckled up and laid the briefcase beside him. The hum of the engines accelerated as it gained power down the runway.

He peered out of the window and watched as the plane lifted leaving the security of the ground below. He didn't mind flying but found it to be boring; the only adrenaline rush was the takeoff and the landing. You would think with all the advanced technology in aviation that flying would only take a matter of minutes, how archaic. Jerry knew this as fact; it was his business to know. Several aircrafts had been built to accelerate the commercial flying time; however, not for the public. The seat belt sign showed off, and he released the buckle.

"Sir, would you like something to drink?" asked Andrew.

"Yes, I'll have a scotch Glenfiddich on the rocks."

"Very good, I'll be right back."

Jerry was not much of a drinker, but when he did drink it had to be the best.

Andrew returned with his drink. "Here you go, Sir."

He took a long sip; it went down smooth.

"Do you mind Sir, if I sit next to you?" asked Andrew.

"No, go ahead." Jerry moved his briefcase.

"Sir, have you heard from Michael?"

"No, it's been awhile."

Jerry took another sip.

"Andrew why don't you pour yourself one of these?"

"No, thank you, Sir. I'm fine. Perhaps Mike hasn't had a chance to call."

"Most likely. Well we know where we're going."

"Maui—is that right Sir?"

"Andrew you are quite right."

ELEVEN

"WHAT'S THE MATTER? WHY aren't you talking to me?" asked Mike.

Sam's eyes remained fixed on the road. "Give me a good reason why I should talk to you?"

"Because this is silly."

Mike waited for a response, and not receiving one he continued. "I'm sorry if that's what you want me to say."

Mike reached for a bottle of water. Sam glanced over at Mike taking a drink; for a brief moment he looked like a child.

"Hey, aren't you going to give me a drink?"

Mike startled by her request, reached for her bottle and handed it to her. "Here you go."

"Thank you. Now that's better, I was thirsty."

"Does this mean you're talking to me now?"

"I think it does. Yes." Sam smiled. "You know it would make it very difficult for you to do our work if I didn't talk to you."

"Sure would. I'm glad we're talking."

"Me too. So, what do you think happened to Tom and Wally? Do you think that they're still following us?"

Sam handed Mike her empty bottle.

"I hope not—I'm really hoping that Makani's friends scared the crap out of them, and they swam all the way back to Maui."

"That would be great if they did. But honestly, I don't think they would give up that easily. Do you?"

"I really hate to say it, but I think you're right."

Mike turned towards the window, absorbing the vast view of the horizon.

"What are we going to do once we get there? I mean are we going to camp or sleep in the jeep?" asked Mike.

"You know you're right. I never thought of that. I'm sure it will take us at least a few days or longer before we put the pieces together."

"Well then we better look into getting some camping gear."

"Agreed, but where? I'm not sure if they even have an outdoor shop."

"I don't know, but we can always Google."

"Here give it a try." Sam handed Mike her phone, and he keyed in the information.

"Doesn't look like it—oh, but wait there is a hardware shop; they might have something. We can go and check it out."

"Where is it?"

"Hmm, let's see…it looks like it's back that way."

Mike pointed behind them.

Sam slammed on the brakes and spun the jeep around."

"Man, warn me when you're going to do that."

Sam laughed. "What's the matter Mike? You look a little white."

"Damn right I am; my stomach's in my throat."

"Well, tell it to get back down," laughed Sam.

"Oh, you're just being a smart ass, aren't you?"

Sam pushed on her stomach "Yup…. down boy!"

"OK, cut the theatrics. We need to focus."

"Aw, you're no fun."

Mike ignored her remark.

"All right then. Hopefully this place is not too far back into town, I don't want to meet up with our dear friends."

"Seriously, I wonder what happened to them."

"Speak of the devil!" said Sam as a black jeep sped past them.

"No way! Are you sure?"

"I'm sure," confirmed Sam.

"Do you think they saw us?"

"I'm not sure. I hope not."

Mike turned around in his seat, confirming that they in fact had not seen them.

"Nope it looks like they didn't. They're still driving up the road."

"Good. Now let's make this quick. Where is this place?"

"Well, according to Google, it should be just around the bend."

"I see it now. It's that little white building just over there."

Sam pulled into the parking lot and they both jumped out of the jeep. Mike held the door open for Sam, and they rushed to the store.

"Doesn't look promising—oh, wait look over there. They do have camping gear."

They walked down the aisle and picked up a couple of sleeping bags, a stackable set of pots, which came in a nice draw string pouch.

"We'll need the small cans of propane," added Mike.

Sam walked up and down the aisle.

"Here they are," shouted Sam, bending down and reaching for two canisters on the bottom shelf. "Do you think this will be enough?"

"No, let's get a couple more." Mike grabbed three more.

"Do we need anything else?"

"A tent? You know that just might come in handy, don't you think?" Mike laughed.

"OK, who's trying to be funny now? Ha... Ha. Anyway, do you see any tents?"

"Here they are." Mike pulled a box off the shelf.

"OK. I think now we're set," said Mike holding the box.

"Um, no. I need one too."

"I thought we would share one tent."

"You would like that wouldn't you? No!" Sam proclaimed with her hands on her hips.

Mike reluctantly grabbed another tent. "Do we have everything now?"

"Almost. We'll need flashlights and a knife. I think that's it."

Mike nodded. As they walked towards the cashier Sam noticed snorkeling equipment.

"What are you planning on doing with that? A little recreational snorkeling?" chuckled Mike.

"Well, you never know, possibly. There is just one more thing we do need and that's food."

"No, we can't forget that. I did see a market down the road."

"Great! Let's get this paid for and grab our eats."

Mike paid the cashier and they loaded up the jeep. They then exited the parking lot and drove down the road to a quaint little market.

"This is nice, and it smells incredible. I want two of everything."

"Hmm, looking at all this food, I just realized how hungry I am," said Sam.

"You too? I know I want it all."

"Oh, guess what we forgot?"

"What?"

"A cooler."

"No, I grabbed it?"

"Really? Where was I? I didn't see you grab it."

"You were busy checking out your snorkeling gear."

"Oh, glad you remembered."

"Well, I can be useful at times."

"That's debatable. Come on, let's get some stuff."

"What did you say?"

Sam smiled and grabbed two grocery baskets, handing one to Mike. "Nothing. I just think we need at least two baskets."

"You're right."

"Let's check out the Deli. Oh, my gosh! Yum! Everything looks amazing."

"I know it does… now what should we get?" Mike looked over the items.

"I think a few salads, and ha everything else," suggested Sam peering into the display.

"I agree with you there!" Mike smiled. "Here let me get these items and you look around for what else you would like."

"Good plan—see you in a bit. Oh, don't forget the chicken."

"I won't."

Sam wandered around and picked up a few more items, and then rejoined Mike.

"Do we have everything?"

"I think all we need is ice and drinks." said Sam

"Water of course, and how about some wine and beer?" said Mike

"Absolutely both—you know a glass of wine would

be nice right about now."

Mike filled his basket with water, wine and beer.

Sam picked up a bag of ice. "Do you think we need more ice?"

"I'll get a couple more, but here let's take this up to the register."

Mike ran back for more ice and Sam unloaded the groceries.

"I think we're done." Mike placed the bag of ice on the conveyor belt, and the cashier handed Mike the receipt. "Mahalo."

"I think this is good for now. We can always come back for more if we need more," said Sam as she helped Mike load the groceries into the jeep.

"Ready to go?"

"I think that's it; let's go," said Mike slamming the door.

Sam drove out of the driveway and stopped, checking each direction before entering the main road.

"Oh no!" Sam just remembered something.

"What? Did we forget something?" asked Mike.

"Yes, clothes, we left in such a hurry I didn't get a chance to grab anything."

"I know it's not like we could have with those two goons after us."

"I wonder if there's a shop close by."

"I'm sure we can find something."

"Let's try up this street—if my memory serves me correctly, I did see a clothing store," suggested Sam.

"There it is," pointed Mike.

"Look, how cute is that it? It's a little hut."

Sam parked and they walked into the store.

"What an adorable store."

"Adorable or not, let's make this quick."

"Mike, look at all these!" Sam immediately gravitated towards the jewelry.

"They are nice, but Sam focus. We need to make this quick."

"Aw alright."

Mike walked over to a swim suit rack.

"Sam here! This looks nice."

"Yes, it does. What size is it?"

Sam searched for the tag. "This should fit; I'll get this. Mike, we do need towels and a few more thing."

"OK, well hurry up. I'll wait outside."

"See you in a bit."

Mike watched from the front entrance making sure that Sam had walked towards the back of the store. He pretended to go through the racks of clothes that were placed on the outside entrance just in case she had happened to look his way. Once he was certain that Sam was occupied, he stepped off the porch and made his call.

"Hello, Jerry. Mike, yeah we're in Lanai. No, we haven't reached the ship yet. I think it'll be awhile before she finds anything once we're there. You're on your way? Well, just chill until I call you with an update."

Mike happened to glance up at the front stoop only to find Sam looking at the rack of clothes. He quickly hid his cell phone and reached for a couple of shirts.

"There you are. What do you think of these shirts and the shorts?"

"I like them both. Nice colors."

"Let me just run in and pay for these."

"Aren't you going to try the shorts on?"

"No, I'm sure they'll fit." While Mike paid for the merchandise, Sam continued to look at the clothes.

"That was quick!" said Sam, surprised.

"I know, I'm quick. Come on, let's go."

Mike handed Sam his clothes as she unlocked the jeep.

"Now where's that road?" Sam asked. "What was it called? Oh, Lanai Avenue?"

"I think it's just down that way."

Sam turned on to the street.

"There's the sign; it says to turn here."

"Good, thanks. Well, here we go."

The road was not without its twists and turns, which made for an interesting ride. The countryside was incredible with its rich red soil like Mars. Indeed, she felt that she was in another world.

"Are we almost there?" Mike asked.

"I think so, it should be just around the bend."

"Mike can you had me my pack?"

"Sure, where is it?"

"Behind my seat."

Mike reached behind the seat and pulled out Sam's pack.

"Here you go, what is it that you wanted?"

"Can you get my lip gloss?" Mike placed his hand into the bag, searching for a small tube.

"Is this it?"

Sam glanced over. "Yes, that's it."

Sam unscrewed the cap exposing a glossy mixture that she rubbed over her lips. Mike watched intently as her lips captured the shimmering rays of the sun. He felt compelled to kiss her but refrained since that would certainly cause another confrontation. Sam replaced the cap and handed the tube back to Mike.

"Hmm, do you think I should try some?" said Mike puckering up his lips.

Sam laughed. "Ha! You might like it. I know it might seem a little vain, but hey a girl can always do with a little help. Oh and I also have a killer of a moisturizer—you should give it a try."

"Me! No, I'll pass. You know you really don't have to use anything; you're a natural beauty."

"Ah, you're sweet."

"Yeah, I know." Mike smiled. "Look at that!" Mike leaned out of the window. The view was spectacular.

"Beautiful view," agreed Sam.

"Sam what do you think the key unlocks?"

"Don't know. At this point we don't even know if it will unlock anything at all."

"This is true."

The jeep angled as it traveled down the rough terrain. Mike held on to the strap which was attached to the side of the jeep for support.

"This road is a little rough!" Mike looked out of the window; the width of the road was narrow with only a foot between the edge and a treacherous leap into the abyss. Sam's concentration was unyielding. They sat in absolute silence. The road seemed to go on forever, until finally the jeep regained its well-balanced state.

"Finally! Now I can breathe!" sighed Mike.

"Me too. That was something—a little shaky, don't you think?"

"My stomach was feeling it. Look there's a spot. We can park there," indicated Mike.

"That does look like a good spot."

Sam parked on an outcrop by the side of the road.

"Look at that!" Mike jumped out of the parked jeep, and ran to edge for a closer look.

"What?"

Sam got out of the jeep joining Mike who was admiring the view.

"It's an old ship! I wonder if that's it."

"I suppose there's no other ship in this vicinity."

Sam wandered around looking for a road that would take them closer to their destination.

"It looks like this is as close as we're going to get. I don't see a road down there."

"I guess we'll have to go the rest of the way on foot," said Mike.

"I guess so. Well, let's unload the jeep."

Mike placed the groceries into the cooler and slung the tents over his shoulder. Sam grabbed their packs and the sleeping bags.

"Do we have everything?" Sam asked, ready to lock up the jeep.

"There's still a few things left, but I'll come back and grab them."

"OK, then let's go."

"Lead the way and I'll follow," said Mike adjusting the tent straps.

"Watch your step, its slippery."

They carefully walked down the embankment as the sea birds dived over their heads, with several near misses. The wind grew blustery at times almost pushing them off the narrow pathway. They began to work in a synchronized rhythm, crouching in unison as the winds full force slammed against their bodies. Once the blustery gale subsided, they continued their descent.

"We're almost there!" called Sam.

Mike said nothing and remained focused on his footing. Sam reached the sandy base.

"Mike, watch it!" Mike ducked in time as a large white seagull swooped past his head.

"Man, what's with these crazy birds? You would think that we were in Alfred Hitchcock's movie *The Birds*!"

"It is strange. I've never seen anything like this."

The pathway was now wide enough for the two of

them to walk side by side down to the beach.

"Where do you think we should set up camp?"

"I'm not sure. Let's see what's around the bend."

The beach was dotted with large boulders that had settled in their sandy graves for millions of years. A large outcrop protruded into the ocean and for them to get to the other side, they would have to get wet.

"Sam here give me your pack."

Sam reached for the straps, unbuckled them, and once loosened handed her backpack to Mike.

They pressed their bodies into the rock face for protection, careful not to be pulled out to sea by the enormous waves. Sam glanced over at Mike ensuring that he wasn't have difficulty balancing the supplies.

"Mike are you all right?"

"I think so."

No sooner had he uttered the words, his foot slipped and forced him to balance the cooler on his hip and grab a piece of protruding rock.

"Mike! Are you all right?"

"Yeah, I'm all right now. That was scary."

Once they reached the other side, they were astonished to find a pristine white sandy beach dotted with several alcoves hidden by grassy knolls.

"This is amazing!" shouted Sam.

"It is! What a great place to set up camp, what do you think?" asked Mike.

"This is a good place—how about right over there?" Sam pointed to a large knoll with an alcove that would serve as protection from the weather.

"That would be perfect!" agreed Mike.

They placed their gear down and took a moment to catch their breath.

"Sam, lets walk down to the shore before we set up."

"OK, let's go. I'm ready."

They stood by the shore looking out on to the vast sea, and there in all its effervescent rustic glory stood the massive Liberty Ship.

"I'm speechless. Are you really going to board that ship?" Mike asked.

"I see no other way, if we're going to find anything. Come on, let's make camp; it's getting late."

"I suppose that's the only way," Mike said. "Well, let's start assembling the tents then I'll run back to the truck and get the other supplies."

"Good idea."

"Then I'll make dinner and we can have that much deserved glass of wine. What do you think?"

"Absolutely! I'm game."

"If we hurry, we can enjoy the sunset too."

"OK. I'll race you."

Mike was the first to start assembling the tent by pulling off the sleeve exposing its structure.

"Sam, can you help?"

"Sure."

Sam grabbed one side of the tent and extended the poles. Mike did the same. With one quick pull the two-man tent was assembled. Mike used a small hammer to secure the pegs into the ground. Sam unraveled the sleeping bags and placed one into the tent.

"There, that looks cozy," said Mike.

"Yes, it does. Now don't you get any ideas."

"What ideas?"

"You know." Sam smiled.

"Hey, I wasn't even thinking about that!"

"Ha! You're funny. Here help me with my tent."

"OK, that was easy. Where do you want it?"

"Not next to you that's for sure. How about just over there to the right and the entrance facing the center."

"Well…OK if that's where you want it."

"Yes, please," smiled Sam.

Once Mike positioned the tent according to Sam's specifications and was absolutely sure that she was satisfied, he unzipped a small bag containing cooking pots.

"Can I help?"

"No, it's OK, I've got it."

Sam looked around and found two large rocks that would work nicely as stools.

"Mike, we can sit on these rocks."

"We can, but we did buy chairs. I'm done for now, so I'll just run back and get the rest of the stuff."

"Do you want me to come?"

"No, just sit and enjoy. Be back in a sec."

She watched as Mike ran up the beach and soon

disappeared. Her attention immediately turned towards the vast ocean with its mysterious anomaly obstructing her view. What hidden secrets will you share—my sweet Liberty?

TWELVE

"THERE'S THEIR JEEP!" exclaimed Wally.

"Yeah, I see it. Let's just park over here so they don't see us."

Tom backed up parking the jeep in a grove of bushes that served as excellent camouflage.

"Let's go!" Wally reached for the door handle.

"No. We'll just wait here a while—just in case they come back to the jeep."

"OK, fine—it's warm in here." Wally rolled down his window.

"At least we have trees to shelter us from the hot sun," said Tom rolling down his window.

"It is a hot one today!" Wally stepped out of the jeep.

"Where are you going? I told you to stay here."

"I need to go…"

"Go where?"

"You know," scowled Wally.

"No, I don't know."

By the look on Wally's face, it dawned on him what he meant.

"OK, but hurry!"

Tom watched as Wally walked behind the truck and then down an embankment looking for a spot to relieve himself.

"For goodness sakes go already!"

Wally turned and gave him the finger.

"What an idiot," said Tom under his breath. He watched as a few vehicles passed by. Wally returned, pulling up his fly.

"Is that better?"

"Much." Wally climbed back into the jeep.

"I wonder what happened to those Hawaiians who were after us?" asked Wally.

"I don't know, and I don't care. I'm just glad we lost them."

"Something tells me that we haven't seen the last of them."

"Well, I hope you're wrong."

Wally wanted to ask Tom what his intensions were once he had caught up to them, but decided against it. He thought it best to keep quiet. If Tom wanted anything more than mere muscle, such as killing them, he would be in for a surprise. That was not what he had signed up for. It was not in his contract, and even if it was he would absolutely not consent to it. Wally reached for a water bottle.

"Hey, can you get me one?"

Wally pulled one out of a bag and handed it to him. "Why are you so into getting Mike anyway? Something tells me that it's not just about the money," said Wally taking a drink.

"You're right. It's not all about the money."

"OK, then what is it?"

"We have a history."

"Really! I'm surprised. What happened?"

"We went to school together."

"What! You did?"

"Yes. High school. We were best friends."

"Best friends? I can't believe that!"

"Well, believe it. It's true."

"OK, then how did you become enemies?" Wally reclined his seat and grabbed his water bottle—this was going to be good.

"Well, where do I start?"

"From the beginning."

"OK, from the beginning. My family had just moved to San Francisco from Calabasas California and we lived next door to Mike and his family."

"I can't believe this; how old were you?"

"I was fourteen and so was Mike. Well, one day as I was walking to school, I noticed a group of boys in front of me. I was hoping that they wouldn't pay any attention to me but unfortunately they did. I was about to cross the street when one of them yelled at me to stop. Before I knew it, he ran in front of me, stopping me dead in my tracks. I tried to act cool and yelled back 'Yeah what? You talking to me?' The leader, I assumed, cracked a smile and said 'Yeah, you! We want to talk to you.' Well, I knew that they didn't want to talk, so I started to slowly edge my way past them, but I was quickly surrounded. They started calling me names and pushing me around."

"Then what happened?" Wally was enthralled.

"The leader threw the first punch and knocked me off of my feet. Before I knew it, each one piled on top of me, taking their best shot."

"Really? Then what did you do?"

"Will you let me finish? I'm getting there. There I was on the ground, blood gushing out of my lip. I was defenseless thinking that I was done for."

Wally sat up in his seat listening intently.

"All of a sudden the beatings stopped. I slowly opened my eyes just in time to see one of the guys being hurled into a thorn bush, then another and another. The rest of the gang ran away. I lay there on the ground, dazed and confused next thing I knew a hand reached down and pulled me up."

"Who was it?"

Tom took a drink and continued. "The stranger asked if I was all right. I tried to keep a brave front. 'Yeah…I'm good.' I said, and then thanked him. He asked me why they were punching the shit out of me and I couldn't give him a straight answer.

'Maybe they just didn't like my looks.'

'Yeah right,' he agreed that I was creepy, rubbed my head and laughed.

Wiping my bloody lip on the sleeve of my jacket,

he asked if I was a new kid.

'Yeah, I was. He then introduced himself as Mike, and from then on we were good friends."

"What? Really? Mike?" Wally couldn't believe it. "Mike? You mean the Mike you're after?"

"Yes, the very same."

"So did the guys bother you after that?"

"No, they would just give us the evil eye every time they saw us. So that's how I came to know Mike."

Tom reached for his water bottle and took a sip.

"I can't believe this—the two of you were friends! What happened next?"

"I eventually did make more friends and with the popular kids at school. Mike fell to the wayside. I mean the tables had turned, and I was the one now protecting him."

"Really? How?"

"Well, the popular kids didn't feel that he was worthy of being in the popular group. I was ridiculed for associating with him."

"Good for you. You stood your ground as to who your friends were."

"Yeah, at the time it felt like the right thing to do."

"What do you mean?"

"Well we remained good friends throughout school and even after the fact, but I soon found out that he was nothing but a user and a backstabber."

"Really? That surprises me."

"Oh Yeah, it surprised me too. So what happened

was one day I came up with this wonderful idea to start my own business."

"What kind of business?"

"I'm getting to that—so I explained the idea to Mike and told him to keep it quiet as it was an idea that would definitely be successful, and he happily agreed. I was an idiot for trusting him because he stole my idea and ran with it."

"Did he succeed?"

"That's when it bites him in the ass and the business didn't pan out. By then I had started another business that had proven to be very lucrative. It was a little shady, but I didn't care since I was raking in the dough. So, when Mike found out how well I was doing he approached me for money. I lent it to him under the condition that he would pay me back with interest."

"That's a twist."

"It turned out that he gambled the money away and had no intention of paying me back."

"So now it's payback time."

"It damn well is! I had found out from my sources that he had borrowed money from them and had paid them back but decided not to reimburse me."

"How did you find out?"

"My sources had also told me that dirty rat had been bad mouthing me all over town. After all that I've done for him! Wally have you ever been betrayed?"

"Me? No, I haven't."

"It definitely hurts you to the core, you become less

trusting. Mike's nothing but a user who finds out what works in your favor and then steals it to make it his own. I may be low, but he's the lowest scum!"

"I see now why you're after him."

"Yup. I want that son of a bitch to pay. He spent years pretending that he was my friend and it was nothing but a charade. I never felt as much a fool as he had made me out to be."

"No one should abuse anyone, let alone a friend in that way."

"True. Yeah, looking back he always made out to be the loner, so I felt sorry for him and stuck up for him. Boy was I a big fool!"

"So, what are you going to do with him once we find him?"

"You'll just have to wait and see."

Wally turned in silence and looked out of the window; if Tom had plans on killing, well he had plans of his own.

"Come on let's go. It doesn't look like they're coming back."

They walked up the path being careful not to be seen.

"Look is that Mike?" said Wally.

"Where?"

"By the truck."

"Yeah, it is. Stay down." Tom pulled on Wally's shirt and they crouched down behind a large bush.

"It looks like they're staying for a while."

"Looks like," Wally agreed.

They watched as Mike pulled out two black bags and threw them over his shoulders. He then slammed the truck door and locked it. Mike soon disappeared out of sight, walking down an embankment.

"So now what do we do?" asked Wally.

"Come on, let's get back to the jeep."

Tom started up the truck. "They won't be going anywhere soon. Let's go back into town and grab a few things. It looks like we'll be doing some camping."

"What! You're not going to confront them?"

"No, not yet. I want to see if they find anything. Then we'll grab them."

"All right, whatever you say."

They drove down the road towards town.

THIRTEEN

"Here you go." Mike handed Sam a plate.

"This looks amazing. When did you become a chef?"

Mike filled his plate and sat down beside Sam. "Me? A chef? No, I just learned how to cook out of shear necessity."

"This is delicious; what spices did you use?"

"Why, thank you. It's pasta with fresh basil and cherry tomatoes and for a little heat some chili."

"Well, I'm impressed. You can do the cooking from now on."

"I don't mind, actually. I was counting on it. I do have our menu planned. Would you like a glass of wine?"

"Absolutely."

Mike reached into the cooler and pulled out a bottle of red wine. Grabbing two glasses, he sat back down. "A little red wine, my sweet?"

"Why yes, I don't mind if I do." Sam held the glasses as Mike poured. "Now for a toast."

"What should we toast to?"

"Well, how about to first love?"

Sam lowered her glass. "Let's just toast to old friends."

Mike hesitated, and then raised his glass. "To old friends."

"This wine is very nice, thank you for getting it."

"It's really not that bad. You're very welcome. Oh, one thing I forgot."

"And what's that?" asked Sam.

"A campfire."

"That would be nice."

Mike assembled a pile of driftwood into the fire pit. Lighting it, it soon burst into flames.

"There how's that?"

"Very nice. Thank you Mike."

"So, I was just wondering how we are going to board the ship?"

Sam took another sip of wine. "Are you a strong swimmer?"

Mike nearly choked on his pasta. "What? You mean we're actually going to swim to the ship?"

"Well, yeah. How else do you expect us to get to get there?"

"Well, you're right I suppose. But I hate to tell you this, I don't know how to swim."

"What? I thought you were a great swimmer."

"No—never learned how."

"Really? I thought you could swim. Didn't we have

a picnic by a lake and go swimming?"

"Yes, we did have the picnic, but don't you remember what happened when you asked me to go for a swim?"

"We went swimming—no wait. Oh no, that's right! You did mention that you couldn't swim, and I made fun of you."

"Exactly!"

"Well, this is not good. I can't believe that after all these years you never took lessons."

"No, I didn't. Never felt there was a reason to."

"Then I guess I'll have to go it alone."

Mike filled their glasses with more wine.

"I'm sorry Sam that I can't be of much help."

Sam took a long drink. "Well I guess you will just have to stay on shore and watch me. Did you get the binoculars?"

"I did. I'll watch your every move, I promise."

"You better. I'll signal to you ever time I reach the ship, so you'll know I'm all right."

"Sam are you mad at me?"

"Mad? No, just disappointed. I might need your help at some point—that's all."

Mike drew closer and placed his arms around her. "I'm sorry babe."

Sam looked into his eyes. The wine was beginning to take effect, and she felt compelled to kiss him. Mike drew even closer placing his lips on hers. Sam hesitated, feeling his warm full lips lightly touching hers. She imagined how nice it would be to feel the pleasure. She hadn't kissed anyone for such a long time.

"Sam…" whispered Mike.

Sam pushed herself away from his seductive grasp. "I think we better call it a night."

"Are you sure you want to?"

"Yes, I think its best. It's been a long day and I want to get an early start."

Mike pulled away." "OK, then if you're sure."

"Yes, I'm sure."

Sam picked up the dishes and dropped them in a bin on her way to her tent.

"Well, goodnight Mike."

"Goodnight. Sweet dreams. See you in the morning."

Sam zipped up her tent. Once she had removed her sweater and sandals, she crawled into her sleeping bag. Her eyes remained fixed on the flickering shadows that danced on the canvas until the fire had diminished into a soft glow.

Mike's ghostly figure bent down stoking the fire, and then he stood and faced her tent. Sam braced herself anticipating his next move, which never happened. Mike had turned and walked towards his tent. Her body relaxed and she closed her eyes. Her thoughts focused on their lips touching, so warm and inviting, and then she drifted off to sleep.

Sam awoke with the smell of coffee in the air and emerged from her tent.

"Good-morning." Mike had made coffee and was pouring her a cup.

"Morning, thank you." Sam cradled the warm cup in her hands before taking a sip. "How is it?"

"Very good, thank you."

"Did you sleep well?"

Sam swallowed. "Yes, actually I did, how about you?"

"Not bad, just kept hearing strange noises."

"Really, like what? I didn't hear anything."

"It seemed to be coming from out there." Mike pointed towards the ship.

"Really? I'm amazed I didn't hear anything at all. I must have been exhausted, I just fell right to sleep."

"I'm sure you were very tired, and the wine might have had something to do with it too."

"Ha! I'm sure that helped." Sam laughed.

Mike filled their cups. "The wine didn't affect me I've always been a very light sleeper, do you remember Sam?"

Sam just chose not to react. Her attention was now focused on the ship.

"When were you planning on going out there?"

"Well, I guess now is as good time as any."

"What now? I was going to make breakfast."

"You know I would really like to get out there. I'll have something to eat once I get back."

Sam stood up.

"OK, if you insist on going, then I'll wait until you get back."

"You can go ahead if you're hungry."

"No, it's OK. I'll wait."

"Well, then I'll just go and get changed."

"You do that. You're right, you know."

"Right about what?"

"Just that you shouldn't eat anything before swimming."

Sam turned and smiled as she walked into her tent. Mike reached into his backpack and pulled out a granola bar, unwrapped it and dipped it into his coffee. He looked at the rusted ship and started to worry, what if she cuts herself? It would be blood poisoning for sure, and there was nothing he could do. For the first time in his life he felt utterly useless. "Sam! Sam!"

"What?" Sam emerged from the tent. "What?"

"I can't let you go out there. What if you cut yourself; you'll get blood poisoning."

"I won't, I'll be careful."

"You better be. Sam I'm so sorry that I can't be there for you."

"I know Mike, but trust me I'll be all right." Sam walked down the embankment towards the beach.

"Hey, wait up!" Mike grabbed the binoculars and followed. Sam threw down her towel and walked into the water.

"Look, do you really have to do this? The waves are huge and it's a long way out."

"Will you stop worrying? I'm a strong swimmer; I'll be fine."

"You better be!"

Sam waited for a huge wave to pass before diving into the water. Mike found a large log close to shore and sat down nervously watching as Sam battled the endless waves that pushed her closer to shore and away from her destination. Suddenly, he lost sight of her. Mike jumped up and ran to the shore. Where is she?

He paced up and down the shoreline hoping to spot her. She must have dove down deep—that's it, thought Mike, trying to avoid the continual plummeting of the waves. He shielded his eyes and scanned the horizon. Come on Sam, where are you?

He finally spotted her within yards of the ship fiercely struggling to conquer the choppy water.

Again, she disappeared. Mike grabbed the binoculars and scanned the water. Suddenly she surfaced and was safely holding on to the ship's porthole.

"I can't believe she did it. She wasn't kidding when she said she was a strong swimmer." said Mike out loud. Relieved, he returned to his log with a tight grip on his binoculars. He was determined to watch her every move.

Sam held on to the porthole as several waves had forcibly sent her under. The swim had proven to be more strenuous then she had anticipated; she was now exhausted. She braced herself as another wave hit pulling her under. Surfacing, she quickly reached up and grabbed on to the top frame of the porthole pulling herself through the opening. Standing on the ledge she was now inside the rusty tomb with the water rushing in below her. She looked up to find that there was an opening to the top of the ship, but how was she going to get there?

She looked around the chamber which was riddled with twisted rusty metal for a way to ascend. On the opposite side of the wall she noticed a ladder made of rope which was intact. Holding her breath, she jumped back into the water and swam towards the ladder.

She reached up and grabbed on to the rope, but her hands quickly slipped and sent her back down into the water. Once again, she tried reaching for it and once again fell into the depths. Her hands were wet, and the diameter of the rope was taxing to grasp; she couldn't get a firm grip. One last try, she thought, and grabbed on to the thick rope with one hand and quickly locked both arms around it.

She began to pull herself up pausing to catch her breath and rest her arms as they were beginning to burn from the rope fibers. Once rested, she ascended through the opening. The top of the ship was scattered with rusty metal, making her exploration a cautious one. How long has this ship been here and why was it here? Suddenly she thought of Mike who must be worried.

She walked over to the starboard side of the ship, and shielding her eyes from the sun she spotted Mike standing on a log looking through his binoculars. She waved and called out to get his attention. He reciprocated. Satisfied, she continued her search for anything that would require a key to unlock. After examining the deck, she was certain that there was nothing that even remotely resembled a locked container that would require a key.

Sam was ready to give up when she noticed several sheets of metal that seemed to be deliberately placed in a corner. Carefully removing the obstacles, she found a small box hidden deep within the crevice. She gently pushed more of the debris out of the way enabling her to get a closer look. She removed the box and upon closer examination found it to be unlocked and empty. Disappointed, she replaced it back into its rightful place.

She continued to look around being careful not to harm herself on any jagged edges. Now she was ready to leave. Her search had proven to be an utter failure. Then something caught her eye just a few inches from her feet. She bent down and moved a piece of debris and found a small box that was locked and fused on to the ship's deck. The box definitely needed a key to unlock it. She reached for her neck, but realized that in her haste she had left the key behind. Nevertheless, she was thrilled with her discovery and was ready to return to the beach.

She walked over to the starboard side and hesitated, debating whether to jump off—it was quite a jump. Examining her sore arms, now scorched with the imprint of the rope, she couldn't bear to return the same way she had come.

Standing on the ledge of the hull, she took a breath and jumped into the water and hit a large wave that catapulted her forward. Surfacing and catching her breathe she could she Mike watching her from shore. She waved, and he waved back.

She took a deep breath and began swimming towards the beach. As she drew closer to the shore, she paused resting for a brief moment. Eyes focused on Mike, who was now jumping up and down screaming, but why? Suddenly she felt something hit her body—it felt like she had just slammed into a brick wall.

Looking around, she noticed the dorsal fin of a shark! He had backed off for a moment perhaps to regain speed to ram her again, but she wasn't going to wait to find out. Taking a deep breathe she dove deep into the water and opening her eyes she could see that he was coming straight for her. Suddenly as if by sheer luck several large waves began to swell. She immediately took advantage by body surfing.

The waves were now aiding her, catapulting her closer and closer to the shore. Terrified that the shark was close behind, she chose not to look for fear that she was about to lose her battle.

"Hurry! Hurry!" Sam could hear Mike yelling at her. She remained focused and kept on swimming until another large wave hit and pushed her right on to the beach. Mike ran over and cradled her wet body.

"Are you OK?"

Sam tried to catch her breath. "I'm... fine."

Mike held on to her as she stood up and they both looked out over the water to see the menacing dorsal fin of the shark disappear into the watery abyss.

"That was too close! Damn you scared me!"

Sam turned looking straight into Mike's eyes. There was something touching about his deep concern for her safety.

"I'm OK. Really I am."

Mike gently wiped the hair away from her eyes. Their eyes locked; his lips touched hers. This time Sam didn't turn away. She welcomed the soft touch of his warm lips on hers.

FOURTEEN

"**B**OY DID I HAVE a rough sleep," said Tom pulling on the lever to adjust his driver's seat.

"Yeah I didn't get much sleep either. Who knew that the stores would close so early?"

"That's for sure; we didn't expect that, but they should be open by now."

Tom started the truck and pulled out of the side road.

"You know I've been thinking," said Wally.

"Really about what?"

"Is the fifty thousand really worth killing them over it?"

"Did I ever say I was going to kill them!" barked Tom.

"What else are you going to do?"

"Rough them up a bit and yeah, maybe do that. This is not just about the money. I told you it's the principle."

"Come on it was a long time ago; you were just kids."

"I don't give a damn! He's going to pay and that's all there is to it! Look are you with me or not?"

Wally sat in silence and glanced out of the window, reevaluating how much he really needed the money.

"I'm paying you good money for this and you know you need it. Feeding your family is not cheap."

Wally slammed his fists on the dash, startling Tom "Fuck you! Don't you ever bring up my family!" Wally leaned into Tom.

"I'm just saying…that's all. You don't have to get angry about it. My mistake. I won't mention them again."

Tom glanced over making sure that Wally had returned to his side of the truck. "So, are you in?"

"Fuck you, yeah I'm in," snapped Wally.

Tom patted Wally's knee. Wally turned and grabbed his arm. "Don't you ever touch me! I'm not your damn friend."

"OK. Just back off!" pleaded Tom.

Wally backed off, sitting as far away from Tom as he could.

"Come on, let's be civil, OK? Hey Wally, come on."

"Yeah whatever, but after this job I don't ever what to see your fucken face on these islands again!"

Tom didn't want to piss Wally off any more than he was. "All right, deal. Now let's get something to eat and get a few things for camping."

"How long do you think we're going to stay out here?" grumbled Wally.

"As long as it takes."

Wally wanted this to be over and forget that he had ever gotten into this line of work. Once it was done, he was definitely looking for a respectable job, one that didn't endanger himself or his family.

"Should we get the food first or the camping gear?" asked Tom.

"It doesn't matter to me; whatever you want."

Tom glanced at Wally and decided not to ruffle his feathers any more than he had to. "Food first?"

"Sure."

The rest of the ride into town was a quiet one, Tom decided to let Wally's anger dissipate before carrying on any conversation. The store was filled with tourists, Tom picked a basket and the two of them walked in different directions. Tom wandered up to the counter and ordered various meats and salads. Wally picked out fruits and water.

"Hey Wally, how about some booze?"

"Go ahead get whatever."

Tom opened a cooler and pulled out a case of cold beer and a few bottles of wine. "How's this?"

"Yeah, good."

"Oh, we can't forget this." Tom grabbed a bottle of rum from off the shelf. "Wally get whatever else you want. I'll meet you up at the register."

Wally wondered around and picked up a few more items.

"Are we done?"

"Need ice. I'll get it."

Tom placed the groceries on the counter while Wally picked up the ice.

Wally found the freezer and pulled out a couple of bags, kicking the freezer shut with his knee. He looked around to see if they had forgotten anything when he noticed that the Hawaiians were also in the store. Wally quickly walked back to the checkout and dropped the bags.

"Hey, look over there."

"Look at what?"

"Look over your left shoulder," whispered Wally.

"Damn, it's them."

They both quickly looked away, careful not to make eye contact.

"Good morning," said the checkout girl smiling.

"Yeah, morning," whispered Tom.

"How is your day going?"

"Good." Damn he had to have a chatty cashier. She scanned all the items but one.

"I need a price check!" she called out.

All eyes were now on them including the Hawaiians. Tom and Wally started to fill the paper bags with grocery items.

"Hey, aren't those the two guys Makani wanted us to scare off?"

"Yeah Brah, that's them."

"Well I guess they don't scare easy."

"That's for sure."

"We'll just have to do a better job of it."

"Yeah man, I guess we do."

"Never mind the price check," said Tom. "I don't want that."

"Are you sure? It would only take a second." Tom pushed the package away from her reach. "No really, forget it."

"OK, then that will be 35 dollars and 28 cents."

Tom pulled out his wallet and threw down 40 dollars. Wally grabbed the bags and they ran out of the store.

"Your change!" called the cashier. They ignored her and ran to the truck.

"Come on let's go!" yelled Tom throwing the groceries into the truck.

Wally jumped in just in the nick of time before Tom threw the truck in reverse and burned rubber down the road.

The Hawaiians were now standing in the parking lot watching as the truck sped away.

"Should we follow them?"

"Yeah, I want to see what they're up to."

"Brah, I wonder… should we call Makani?"

"No, let's follow them around first and see what's going on."

"OK, well let's go."

Four of them jumped into their black low ride truck, two up front and two in the back, and sped on to the road.

"I think they went that way."

"Yeah, I saw them. We'll just follow, but not too close. I don't want them seeing us.

"We'll surprise them, right?"

"We'll see what Makani wants us to do."

"For sure, Brah."

"Do you see them?" Wally turned around in his seat.

"No, I don't. I don't think they're following us."

"I'm not sure about that, but let's get our camping stuff and get the hell out of here."

"There's the store." Tom turned right into the parking lot.

"Let's make this quick. Sleeping bags, a cooler, a few lamps, and binoculars."

"Good I'll get the bags and binoculars."

"I'll get the rest and let's meet up at the cash register." Tom walked down one aisle and Wally the other. Tom grabbed the supplies and walking to the cashier, he noticed knives. He paused and then decided on a hunting knife.

"What do we need that for?" asked Wally who was standing right behind him.

"You never know when it will come in handy."

Wally raised his eyebrows as they walked to the register and paid the cashier.

"OK, we're all set. Let's go." They threw their gear into the back seat and drove out of town.

"Did you see that?" said one of the Hawaiians.

"Yup, it looks like they're planning a little camping trip."

"Where do you think they're going?"

"Where does every tourist go? Shipwreck Beach."

"Well, there could be other places you know," said the third Hawaiian.

"Brah, I know, but we'll check the beach first and if they're not there I'm sure we won't have trouble finding them on this island."

"That's for sure. So what are we going to do?"

"Brah, what do you think we're going to do? We're going camping?"

A voice from the back seat spoke up. "Then crap, we need stuff Brah. We can stop at my house; it's not far from here. That way we can get some Ka mea ai."

"We just ate nui nui. Is food all you ever think about Brah?"

FIFTEEN

"MIKE WHAT ARE we doing?"

"I think it's called kissing."

Sam pulled away. "This can't happen."

"Why? You must admit it was nice."

Sam walked back up to their campsite.

"Yes, I'll admit it was nice, but it just can't happen again! Do you understand?" She wrapped a towel around herself.

"No, I don't understand. Perhaps you could explain it to me?"

"Because what was between us is now long gone and I don't want to go down that road again."

"Come on Sam, what was so bad about our relationship? Tell me! I was under the impression that it was wonderful."

Sam pulled on her shorts over her bathing suit and grabbed a T-shirt. "It was and that's exactly it—past tense."

Mike grabbed a bottle of beer out of the cooler. "Do you want one?"

"No…I mean yes. You've got me all confused."

"Well, I wouldn't want to do that. Here you go. Now explain to me why you don't want to get involved?"

Sam took a sip. "Because it's been a long time, and we were just kids and sorry now my priorities have changed."

"Your priorities or your feelings towards me?"

"OK, I'll be brutally honest."

"Please do."

"When we first started dating, yes, I fell deeply in love with you, but as time passed I felt that I wanted more."

"More? Like what? A deeper commitment?"

"No, I wanted more in my life—not to be just a good little wife with kids and the white picket fence."

"OK, go on."

"I felt that I needed to prove to myself and the world that I had something of value to offer or to contribute in some way."

"And you couldn't do it with a partner?"

"No. How can I explain this without hurting you?"

"Try me."

"Well, I always had a feeling that I needed someone who was not content with just settling, someone who could evolve in all areas of his life."

Mike took a long drink. "And you never saw that in me?"

"No. I'm sorry, I didn't. All I could see was a man

who was very content with what life had tossed him and was not inclined to grow as a person."

"So I was not up to Samantha's high standard, right?"

"Right? No…but then again, yes. You're confusing me again."

"Wow I never realized how conceited—"

"Conceited? Hey! That has nothing to do with it!"

"Doesn't It? You think that you're better than me. I can't believe this!"

"You're missing the point. I loved you and respected you for who you are, which was a big part of my life back then. Your love taught me a lot, but it was our first love and would be the groundwork for the bigger picture."

"Groundwork! Are you for real?"

"Listen to me. You can't deny that the statistics for first love to work out as lifetime partners are very low. However, it is meaningful for our future love relationships."

"You know what? I really don't know you."

Sam held up her empty beer bottle, indicating she wanted more. "Does anyone? Come on, can't we just be friends?"

Mike handed her a beer.

"Thanks. Look Mike, I know who I am and what I want. Can you honestly say that you know?"

"OK, you got me. I don't want to talk about this anymore."

"Hey, there's nothing wrong with not knowing

yourself or what you want—it's learned as we go through life. But you see I have always known—call it an inner voice. And that being said, I need a partner that has all the attributes I need, so that we can thrive as a couple."

"OK. I get it!"

"I have always known this in my heart and in knowing I admit that I've made it very difficult for me to commit to just anyone."

"I guess we're going to continue talking about this. So now I'm just anyone?"

Sam gave Mike a look

"Sorry…go on."

"I always felt that there was something better for me just around the corner."

"What if better never comes and you never find him?"

"Then I'll just have to be content with being alone."

"Samantha in all my years of knowing you I never really knew you at all."

"Yeah, well at that time of my life I only knew bits and pieces of myself but not the full picture."

"So, where do we go from here?"

"Let's make a toast to our rekindled friendship—to friends for life. How do you feel about that?"

"Well, you're not giving me much of a choice. It's either friendship or I lose you for life, and if that's the case then I choose friendship. As long as you can guarantee it will be for life."

"Absolutely! Guaranteed. Cheers!" Sam held up her bottle.

"Cheers! So did you find anything on the ship?"

"I found a couple of things, but I need to go back in the morning."

"What back? Really? It's too dangerous—you almost got devoured by a shark."

"That was a close call, but I need to go back and look around some more."

"How can you return without endangering yourself?"

"There really is no other way, a raft? And we don't have one."

"Well, let's get one."

"No, forget it. We'd be only wasting time, I'll just take my chances."

"I suppose I could always wade in and tease it into biting me."

Mike walked over to the camp stove, chuckling.

"You know that might not be a bad idea."

"Hey, I was just joking."

"No, it is a good idea. If the shark shows up again you can cause a commotion in the opposite area. That way it buys me time to get to the ship. Bear in mind it's only if he shows up."

"Do you really think that would work?"

"Don't know, but it's definitely worth a try."

"Sam it's a crazy idea, but you know if it keeps you safe, then I'll do it."

"Thank you—that means a lot. Oh, and as added protection I know what else I can do. It might sound a little out there, but it can't hurt. It's an old Hawaiian custom of praying to the sharks for safety."

"Hmm, you can do that?"

"Yes, I think I can. I've witnessed several of Makani's prayer sessions in his lectures, which by the way are truly amazing."

"I'm sure they are, but can you actually keep them away from you?"

"At this stage of the game anything is worth a try. You know that's what I love about the Hawaiians their respect for all life, whether threating or not."

"If that's what you want to do go ahead, but first are you hungry?"

"Actually, yes."

"You just sit back and do what you do, and I'll make us lunch."

"Well, all right, kind Sir."

"How's about hot dogs?"

"Funny, I was just craving them. How did you know?"

"Ha! I just did, and you say we are not meant for each other?"

"You're crazy," smiled Sam. Can I help?"

"No, just sit and relax. I've got this."

Mike pulled out the camp stove and fired it up.

"If you really don't need my help, then I'll just take a walk down to the beach."

"OK, I'll call you once they're done."

Sam walked down to the water's edge and stared at the ship. Its ghostly shell had her mesmerized. What unseen dark secrets had she captured, and would she allow her secrets to be exposed to the light.

Sam was now deeply involved in discovering her magic. Her attention was focused on the box. Would the key actually unlock it, and if it did what would she find?

Her intuition was telling her that something wasn't right—finding the box was far too easy. Someone went to great pains to hide the key, and for the box to be out in plain sight just didn't make sense. She concluded that there must be another box. Her search would continue.

"Sam!"

"Yeah Mike," shouted Sam as she walked back up to the campsite.

"Lunch is ready."

"OK. Coming."

"Here you go." Mike handed Sam a paper plate along with a glass of wine.

"No, the wine will have to wait until later, but the hot dog looks good."

"I guess it is still early for that. I'll get us a couple of waters. I hope you like the works on your dog?"

"I sure do."

"Here you go. Your bottle of water."

"Thanks." Sam didn't realize how hungry she was and took several bites. "This hits the spot."

"It sure does."

"So, tell me your plans for tomorrow."

"Well tomorrow—early in the morning, I'll do the protection prayer and hope for the best. Then I'll swim back out to the ship."

"All right, but I won't lie; I'm scared for you."

"Don't worry, I'll be fine. But you know something is bugging me."

"What's that?"

"Well, I did find a box on deck."

"Really you did?"

"Yes, I did, but it just seems that it was placed in a far too obvious area. I don't think it's the right box."

"Do you think there's another?"

"Possibly. I'll look around some more tomorrow. "You know this is delicious."

"Do you want another?" Sam took her last bite, and smiled.

"Yup you do. I'm on it." Mike got up to prepare a couple more hot dogs.

"Here you go. Are you sure you don't want a glass of wine?"

"Hmm, OK. Twist my arm."

Mike handed her a glass.

"Thank you. You know you would make a great waiter."

"Oh, no!"

"No, really have you ever considered that line of work?"

"Sam, how can I put this in words—hell no!"

"Hey, there's nothing wrong with being a waiter."

"No, there isn't if you're into that kind of profession, but it's not for me." Mike elbowed Sam.

"Funny man. So then what is your kind of profession?"

"Not sure, but I am learning to like archeology all over again."

"Really? That surprises me." Sam stood up. "Are you done?"

"I am."

"Here let me take your plate it's the least I can do." Mike handed her his plate."

"So tell me, why would it surprise you?"

"Your sudden interest in archeology? You've said that you were never interested."

"Back then it was different. I hated the teacher."

Sam turned towards Mike. "Ah I see, and I take it that's the root of your problem for not finishing your education."

Mike smiled. "I suppose it could be. It all depends who's teaching."

"You're incredible you know," smiled Sam.

"I know I am. Come on. Let's go for a walk."

"Sounds good. Which way?"

"How about this way up the beach?"

"I can't believe I've never been to this island before! It's definitely a hidden gem."

"I thought you would have worked on all of the islands."

"Funny you would think so, but no just mainly on Maui and Oahu. Well, I'll tell you one thing I will definitely be coming back. It's so tranquil and so secluded away from the busyness of the other islands."

"Agreed," said Mike stepping over a piece of driftwood.

"It's sad that it's all due to progress. Do they not understand the importance of retaining the very fabric of traditional ways that have been around for centuries? Ways that respect all life on Earth not just mankind. With the rapid acceleration of progress, the very essence becomes lost to a population that no longer cares."

"Exactly Sam, and let's not throw money into the equation."

"There's really nothing wrong with money and power, it's how it's being used and who processes it. Now changing the subject, tell me something, why haven't you learned to swim."

"That came out of left field! I was expecting more deep conversation."

"I decided to lighten it up a bit."

"That you have. I just never really wanted to."

"Are you afraid of the water?"

"Me? No, I'm just not into it."

"Really? You're not" Sam tripped Mike and pushed him into the water, laying him flat on his back.

"Ha! Now you're into it!" laughed Sam.

Mike swallowed the salty brine as a wave pelted his body.

"Oh man, you're in trouble now!" Mike grabbed Sam and pulled her down on top of him.

"Hey, what are you doing?" Sam struggled to get away from Mike's grasp.

"Pay back."

"OK, you got me good. Here let me give you a hand."

Sam pulled Mike up on to the shore. "You must admit, the water felt pretty good."

"Yes, it did. I was surprised at how warm the water is, just like bathwater."

"I know, don't you just love it? Come on, race you back!"

Sam ran towards the camp and Mike tried keeping up with her until she suddenly stopped in her tracks.

"You're pretty fast. Why did you stop?"

"Look is that someone in our camp?"

"Shit yeah. Hey, what are you doing?" Mike yelled.

The two men realized that they had been spotted and ran up the embankment and into the bushes. Mike tried running after them but lost them in the thick brush.

"Damn look at this mess!" The camp had been ransacked.

"It definitely looks like they were looking for something," said Mike.

"The key!" Sam ran into the tent. "Thank God, it's still here!"

"That's a big relief!" Mike started to rearrange the campsite.

"Look at this place! Did they take anything at all?"

Sam assisted Mike in the cleanup.

"No, it doesn't look like it. Most likely they were just looking for your key."

"Thank goodness, they didn't find it—this baby is going to stay with me."

"What are you doing?"

Sam found a piece of rope that had been laying in the sand. Obviously discarded by a passerby. She frayed it and placed the string through the key hole.

"Here, Mike can you tie this around my neck?" Sam handed him the string. "Tie a couple of knots; I don't want it falling off."

"Done. I'm sure you won't lose this. It's on tight."

"Thank you. Now, I really need that glass of wine. They didn't take that did they?"

"No, thank goodness. I've got a bottle right here."

Mike poured them a glass.

"Thanks. Who do you think they are?"

"Who else could it be, but Tom and his muscle Wally?"

"That's just great! We definitely don't need them in our way."

"You're telling me."

"In case they do come back I don't think we should sleep in separate tents tonight."

"What?" Sam almost choked on her wine.

"If they come back there's no telling what they'll do, and I don't want to take a risk on you being hurt."

"Do you really think that they are capable of that?"

"At this point, he's desperate," said Mike, "and I wouldn't put it past them.

"Well, if you think we should double up, then OK. But just keep your hands to yourself. Promise? Mike promise?"

"OK, I promise, friend." Mike smiled.

SIXTEEN

"**T**HAT WAS CLOSE." TOM tried to catch his breath.

"That was. Do you think they saw us?"

"I'm sure they did. I need to sit." Tom unlocked the truck, leaving the door open and sat down. "There that's better."

"Did you get the key?" asked Wally.

"No, couldn't find it. Either they had it on them, or it was still in the camp somewhere."

"Hey, what are you going to do with the key when you do find it?"

"Don't complicate matters. I was going to figure that out once I had it."

"Man, you're some weird Brah." Wally walked away.

"Where are you going?" asked Tom.

"I need to get away from you for a while."

"You're coming back right? Hey, you are right?" yelled Tom.

Wally raised his hand in agreement as he

disappeared into the brush. Tom lay back and closed his eyes, taking a cat nap.

"Wally is that you?" Tom awoke with a start, certain that he heard Wally. Looking around Wally was nowhere in sight. The wind had picked up and the brush began to sway wildly. Tom exited the truck slamming the door only to have the wind blow it open.

"Wally, where are you?" Receiving no answer, he walked deeper into the brush. "Wally!"

Still no answer. Where did he go? Tom could feel a sense of panic set in. The wind speed had accelerated faster than he anticipated, making it very difficult to maintain his balance.

"Wally!" Again, no answer. He was beginning to think that any attempt at yelling out for him would be futile with the deafening sounds. The skies grew increasingly dark and it was soon after that he found himself in complete darkness. His panic now heighted as he desperately searched for his way back to the vehicle. With his arms outstretched he grabbed on to the blades of tall grass for balance, only to have his hands cut in the process. Cradling his bloody wounds, he suddenly found himself on the ground and shielded his head to protect him from any impending blow.

"Hey, what the hell are you doing?"

Tom could barely make out the words through the roaring wind. He released his grip slightly as he could feel his body being lifted from off the ground.

"Are you OK?" asked Wally as he stood over Tom.

"Who are you?"

"It's me, Wally. Who else?"

Tom relinquished his grip as Wally assisted him in regaining his balance.

"Did you see that?"

"See what? What are you talking about?"

"The darkness!"

"I still don't know what you're talking about. It's a beautiful clear day in the middle of the afternoon."

"No, it was extremely windy. Didn't you feel it? Then it grew so dark that I couldn't see anything."

"Man, you're on something. Come on, let's get back to the truck. I'm hungry."

Tom was disorientated, stumbling as he followed Wally. Once out in the open Wally turned to see if Tom had followed. There was no sign of him, Wally started to feel a little worried and sorry for the jerk. He would give it a few minutes, and then go back and look for him. After a few minutes passed and no Tom, Wally returned to the brush only to find that Tom had finally emerged.

"Well, it's about time. I thought you would never come out."

Tom was definitely in need of help. Wally ran over and grabbed his arm and helped him to the truck. The guy was a jerk, but in his books he was not beyond compassion.

"Man, are you OK?"

"I think so."

"Here, I'll get you some water." Wally reached into the back seat and handed Tom a bottle of water, unscrewing the cap for him.

Tom downed the whole bottle.

"Wow, you were thirsty!"

Tom handed Wally the empty bottle. "Can I have another?"

"Easy man we don't have that many."

Tom wiped his lips dry.

"So, tell me what happened."

"I decided to go look for you and suddenly the wind picked up and the further I walked into the brush the windier it got and before I knew it the sky had turned pitch black and I couldn't see anything. As I was fighting the gusts, I cut my hands—I think on the blades of grass. Tom held out his hands for Wally to see.

"I see nothing; just your hands."

"No, no, see the cuts—they're right here."

Tom displayed the palms of his hands only to see that there was nothing.

"What? No, this can't be. I know they were bleeding."

Wally began to worry. "Well if there were cuts, then they're gone now."

"How can this be? No, no they were here."

"Maybe you were dreaming."

"No…wait I did fall asleep when you left, but how did I get into the brush?"

"I don't know maybe you're a sleepwalker."

Tom wasn't accepting Wally's explanation, but he decided to agree.

"Yeah maybe, maybe you're right."

"Of course, I'm right." Wally slapped Tom on the arm. "Are you hungry?"

"Yeah, I am."

"Good, you just sit back, and I'll make us something to eat."

"Yeah, OK, but I'm still feeling a little off."

Wally started to unpack the provisions they had purchased in town and moved them into the clearing just behind the truck. Once finished, he glanced over at Tom only to see that he hadn't moved at all and was still sitting in the same position. Something about Tom was making him feel uneasy, and he had no idea what it was.

Tom stared into the horizon appreciating its beauty as if for the first time. He sat motionless for what seemed like an eternity.

"Tom! Tom!" Wally called waiting for him to react. As he watched Tom's back transform from a lifeless form into the familiar mannerisms that he was used to seeing, Tom sprang into action and jumped out of the truck.

"Yeah? Wally what?"

"Food's ready."

Tom walked over to the camp stove and peered in. "This smells incredible. What is it?"

"It's just hamburger helper."

"It sure smells good."

"Here." Wally handed him a plate. Tom filled it and sat down on a log.

"Slow down. You're eating too fast."

"It's just so good."

"Well great. Go on and enjoy."

Tom added more food on to his plate.

Wally couldn't stop staring at him. "Are you OK?"

"Me? Yeah, why shouldn't I be?"

"No, it's just that you're acting a little strange."

"Why because I'm hungry? Haven't you seen anyone eat before?"

"Hey, it's all good as long as you're feeling all right."

"Never better," said Tom as he took another bite.

"So, have you thought of what we're going to do, once we get the key?"

"What key?"

"You know the key that unlocks the treasure."

Tom paused holding his fork in midair.

"You know. The treasure that might be on the ship?" repeated Wally.

"What ship?"

Wally was puzzled, why couldn't he understand what he was saying? "You know the ship! Mike…remember?"

"Oh, oh yeah. I remember now." Tom stood up and lifted the lid of the cooler and grabbed a water bottle.

"We'll watch what they do and then board the ship once they're on it."

"Oh, I see. If that's what you think we should do."

Wally watched as Tom pulled out another water and downed it.

"Can you pass me a beer?"

Tom appeared puzzled as he leaned over the cooler searching for a beer.

Wally stood up and reached into the cooler and pulled out a beer.

"It's OK I have one."

"Oh, good." said Tom.

Wally took a long drink. Something was definitely wrong, and his suspicions were certainly making him feel uneasy.

SEVENTEEN

"RAMSAY! YOU MADE IT. I didn't think you would. Where were you hiding? I didn't see you at takeoff."

"Have you ever known me to miss a flight? What took you so long?"

"I didn't see you when we boarded."

"I was hiding in the cockpit. These rookie pilots need to be shown a few tricks from the best."

"And that would be you, I assume."

"Damn right. I'm the best damn pilot around," bragged Ramsay as he fastened his seat belt.

"Well, you know I can't argue that," agreed Jerry.

"So what do you do for a drink around here?"

"Andrew! Can you get us two scotches on the rocks?"

"Yes Sir."

"Very good old man, you remembered," smiled Ramsay.

"How can I forget?"

"Aw yes, we did have some good times."

"We did at that."

Andrew returned with the drinks.

"Cheers."

"This is so smooth, unlike the rot we used to drink," chuckled Ramsay.

"Yup, that was pretty bad stuff." Jerry unlocked his briefcase.

"So you were vague when we spoke, where are we flying to?" asked Ramsay.

"Our destination is an island in the South Pacific called Lanai, but we will be flying to Maui first."

"Hmm isn't Lanai the island where the Navy towed that WWII ship—what was it? The Liberty?"

"No, it's actually a World War II YOGN-42, but everyone thinks it's a Liberty."

"True. If I recall correctly, it was left on Shipwreck Beach."

"Exactly."

"So why are we going there?" asked Ramsay.

"Well, it seems that a key to an experiment that we were conducting has been found."

"What key? What experiment? Refresh my memory."

Jerry pulled out the official papers.

"In 1960 the government conducted a secret experiment using the ship as a conductor to create a wormhole. We had secretly equipped the ship into a research vessel. The public assumed that it was just placed there to rot, which was a great cover for our use."

"Ingenious, right under their noses," said Ramsay, taking a drink.

"Exactly. What better way to conduct a plan in secret, but to be so blatantly obvious that the public won't deem it as being suspicious."

"It isn't the first time we've done this." Ramsay raised his glass.

"You and I both know that for a fact. Cheers."

"Why was this area in particular chosen?"

Jerry lowered his glass. "It was chosen due to the unusual storms that would suddenly appear out of nowhere and the ship was continuously being hit by lightning strikes. In doing so it made it easy to capture the high voltage that was needed."

"Interesting."

"There's more. A civilian by the name of Milton Underwood found this to be very usual, and he was working on a theory that electricity given the proper elements would be able to tear a hole in the atmosphere, thus creating a man-made wormhole."

"Incredible! How did you find him?"

"It was easy. He came to us with his hypothesis and we took a great interest."

"That was convenient. Did he have any terms or conditions? Did he ask to be paid an exorbitant amount?"

"Strange, no he didn't. All he did ask for in return was for his family to join him in his study and once the experiment was complete and successful, he wanted to take the credit."

"And you agreed of course," smiled Ramsay.

"Of course." Jerry replaced the documents into the briefcase and locked it.

"Hmm, and with no intention of ever giving him the credit?"

"Naturally. You know the drill," said Jerry.

"Oh, all too well."

General Ramsay sat back enjoying his drink. Once done, he held up his glass for a refill. Andrew noticed and retrieved his glass.

"OK now carry on. What happened next?"

"Apparently he did receive more than a signal."

Ramsay leaned closer. "What? Really?"

"Yes, his last communication with us was as he put it, 'I have contact with beings that are not of this world. They have come through the hole that I have activated.'"

"This is very interesting indeed! Is that all he said?"

"He did mention that he had created a key from a piece of a meteorite he had found on the beach, and when he placed it in the transmitter it was activated. No other metal that he had forged to make the key had produced such favorable results."

"Astonishing. So are we going to meet up with him?"

"Afraid not. We lost all communication with him. A hurricane hit the island and unfortunately he and his family perished."

"Pity. So the project was scrapped. Then why are we going there?"

"Well, I was hoping that once the family had met their demise the project would have been closed. However, the government decided that since the key had never been found it would be wise to remain alert, in the event that it was ever found. So as a precaution, I at random intervals would send an insider out on the field and he or she would report back to me if anything had been discovered. Well, on this occasion my informant contacted me and surprisingly the key has been found in a small metal box."

"Really where? That would defiantly be a reason to reopen the investigation."

"Absolutely, it was found at a dig site by a local archaeologist by the name of Samantha Woods. And if she gets a little too curious and happens to put two and two together, then there's no telling what could happen."

"Do you think she's capable of doing so?"

"Highly unlikely; however, we are not taking any chances that she might accidentally activate it."

"So then this makes for an exciting adventure."

Jerry took a long sip. "You understand the importance of this assignment?"

"I certainly do. Hasn't the government already been in contact with aliens in area 51 and other facilities?"

"Yes, they have. They have even gone so far as to

set up a meeting with them."

"I do vaguely remember that they were in the midst of organizing it at the time."

"They did and apparently a secret deal was reached."

"Fascinating. What kind of deal?"

"That is top secret and I was not privy to the outcome."

"It's just like them to not give anyone the truth. Leave it up to the public to draw their own conclusions. And by the government not responding to either side of an assumption it does not vindicate them in any shape or form."

"Well, they do what they do, and my duty is to concentrate on the ship at hand."

"Well, then. This should be relatively easy. All we have to do is get the key and clean up any evidence of the project." replied Ramsay.

"Correct," affirmed Jerry."

"Cheers to that."

"So how about some food? All this official talk has made me hungry."

"I can use something myself. Andrew!"

"Yes Sir."

"General Ramsay and I are ready for dinner now."

"Very good, Sir. It will be ready shortly."

EIGHTEEN

S AM AWOKE WITH THE smell of bacon frying. She threw on her sweater.

"Well good-morning, sleepy head."

"Morning, where's the coffee?"

"It's ready, it's right there."

Sam wandered over and filled her cup.

"So how did you sleep?"

"Not very well."

"Why? I didn't lay a hand on you." Sam sat on a log cradling her coffee.

"It wasn't because of you. You did keep your promise."

Mike joined her. "So, what is it then?"

"I had that dream again."

"Oh, yeah that would be disturbing enough to keep you up."

"This time there was something different."

Mike stood up to stir the eggs. "Really, how's that?"

"That's the problem; I can't remember."

"Here you go." Mike handed her a plate. "Have

something to eat maybe it will refresh your memory."

"Since when does food refresh one's memory?"

"I don't know. It just might help."

"Hmm." Sam took a bite. "This is really good."

"Good, because I made plenty."

Sam refilled her plate. "After breakfast I thought I'd swim out to the ship again."

"Really! Do you want to?"

"Hey, I have to—remember? That's why we're here."

"I know. I don't need to be reminded, just worried that's all."

Sam stood up and grabbed his plate. "I'll be fine, I'll give that prayer for protection a try—it can't hurt."

"Absolutely. I'll pray too. I really hate it that you're doing this all alone."

"Well you can't swim and unless you're a real quick learner, there's nothing much we can do."

"Aw, I'm quick at a lot of things, but not that quick when it comes to learning to swim."

"Yeah. Well, you work on that. I'm going down to the beach."

Sam grabbed a plastic bag on her way down and placed it in her bra.

"What are you going to do with that? Bag a shark?" joked Mike.

"Ha, oh man, you really need some help you know."

"Yes, that I do, and you're the only one who can

help me. Do you want me to come?"

"No, I'd rather be alone." Sam walked down to the shore. Facing the ship, she closed her eyes and outstretched her arms, palms facing up. She tried to remember the protection chant and couldn't. Instead she made up her own. "Blessings to the seas, the animals that swim within, Blessings to the life it provides, Blessings to the life it creates, Blessings to the power it holds, Blessings to the protection that surrounds me. Mahalo blessings," concluded Sam, imaging the ocean covered in a blanket of pink, which was love.

"Sam! Are you done?" shouted Mike.

She slowly turned, disappointed that her focus had been broken. "I'm done."

Mike ran down to the shore and joined her. "So now what?"

Sam took off her shorts and T-shirt revealing her bathing suit. "I'm going in."

"What now? I thought you'd wait a bit."

"No, I want to do it now."

She walked into the ocean; gentle waves began caressing her legs.

"OK, if you insist. I'll watch you. I'll be right here sitting on this log."

"You do that and remember if you see our shark."

"I'll be the decoy," said Mike, secretly wishing he wouldn't have to resort to that.

Sam jumped into the waves, disappearing quickly into the depths beneath. The surf had changed from calm to choppy, which was a concern. The shark could suddenly appear with no warning. The locals were quite adamant about not going into the water when it was choppy. Choppy made the waters cloudy and anything could be mistaken for food. They would also frequent dangerously close to the shoreline. Sam surfaced and she was amazed at the distance she had achieved.

She managed to swim within a few feet of the porthole. Despite its close proximity, the waves were proving to be taxing. She took a moment to rest before continuing. Once the waves became tolerable, she continued, reaching the porthole in a matter of minutes. She now reached up, but her hand slipped throwing her back into the water.

As soon as she resurfaced, she glanced over at the shoreline to wave at Mike who was trying to get her attention by displaying a series of erratic movements. What is he doing? Her eyes focused on the waves that were growing increasingly larger as each one surpassed the last. It wasn't until the last wave passed that she understood why Mike was in such a frenzy—a shark had surfaced and was heading right towards her.

She reached for the porthole but once again slipped into the waters below. Her heart pounded with such an intensity that she was certain it would explode. Quickly she reached up and managed to get a firm grasp on the wet steel and pulled herself into the entrance. She watched below as the shark bumped into the side of the ship, then disappeared as quickly as it had appeared.

Glancing over to the shoreline she waved at Mike, confirming that she was safe.

Taking a moment to catch her breath, she then followed her previous route into the hull. This time she felt her strength intensified by her determination and the adrenaline rush from the shark. The result was an effortless climb. Now that she was on deck, she signaled Mike from the starboard side by waving. Mike on the shore waved back. Satisfied, the next point of business was to try the locked box.

Sam removed the string from around her neck and placed the key into the opening. Anticipating the result, she turned the key, but the box did not open. She was now having difficulty trying to remove the key from the lock.

"Damn it!"

All she needed was for the key to snap off. So now what? Taking a deep breath, she tried once again and managed to extract it without damaging it.

"Thank goodness."

With the key in hand she looked around for something that would require a key. Feeling defeated and ready to leave, suddenly she was startled by a loud bang and froze.

Reluctantly, she slowly turned fearing the worst. Her eyes immediately were drawn to the box, which to her surprise was now open. She approached with caution. There was nothing that could have opened the stubborn box on its own, unless she had mistakenly unlocked it while trying to free the key.

The contents were minimal with the exception of a map of what looked like the constellations. Puzzled, she placed the map into her plastic bag and tucked it in her bra. Turning to leave she had failed to notice that hidden beneath the map was an imprint of the key. Excited with her find she removed her key and carefully placed it on the imprint, which was an exact match.

She stepped back anticipating a monumental outcome that sadly didn't occur. Disappointed, she decided to leave the key in its box for safe keeping and return to shore. Satisfied with her decision, she walked to the starboard side of the ship and looked along the shoreline to wave at Mike. To her surprise, Mike was nowhere to be seen.

"Where is he?" her voice reverberated in the iron ship.

Sam decided to abort any further search. Getting back to Mike was her priority. After assessing the ocean waves, she jumped into the depths below. Once she reached the shore after a hard swim, it was all too obvious what had happened to Mike. He was being restrained by Tom and his companion Wally.

"Well, now look at what the waves have washed in—a mermaid! Wally get her!"

Sam quickly tried running away only to be tackled to the ground by Wally who grabbed her by the arm and dragged her up the beach.

"Well, now isn't this cozy."

"Let her go you asshole! You want me; she's got nothing to do with this!"

"Oh, I think you're wrong, she has a lot to do with this," said Tom.

"I'll give you the money," pleaded Mike.

"Yeah, well that might have worked before, but now that I know you're hunting for treasure, it just makes it a little more interesting."

"What treasure? There's no treasure!"

Tom punched Mike in the stomach causing him to double over. "Don't take me for a fool. I know all about it."

"Yeah? You know shit!" gasped Mike.

"Actually, you know I've been thinking—"

"You think? Don't flatter yourself," snapped Mike.

Tom bent down and unearthed a machete that he had hidden in the sand. "So you think I'm a dumb shit, hey? Tom shook the machete in Mike's face forcing him to lean back. Wally braced himself ready to intervene if things escalated.

"Come on now—back off!" shouted Mike.

"You don't think that I'll do it, hey? Well, I wouldn't hesitate."

Tom lowered the knife. "Now tell me where the treasure is!"

"It's over there you shit!" Mike turned his head towards the ship.

"What out there?"

"Yeah, go and get it! It's waiting for you."

"Well, it better be. Wally watch them!"

Wally grabbed Mike, loosening his grip on Sam, who took immediate action and ran towards the beach and jumped into the water. Tom followed. Mike and Wally watched as Tom persistently tried to keep up with Sam's pace, but failed. Sam surfaced to see that Tom despite his lack of swimming skills was making headway. She decided to dive deep into its depths and circle back to shore.

"What's that?" yelled Tom as he felt a sudden bump on his left side. He looked around the surface of the water and spotted a dorsal fin coming straight for him.

"Sam! Hurry!" yelled Mike.

Sam turned to see the fin accelerating in Tom's direction. Behind her a large wave was forming, and its timing was never more impeccable. Bracing herself in her body surfing stance, she was carried right on to the beach.

"Are you OK? Man were you ever lucky!" Mike leaned down and pulled her exhausted body up further on the beach.

"I'm fine—where's Tom?" asked Sam.

"I don't think Tom was as lucky," said Wally pointing to the ocean.

The ocean which was once azure was now stained crimson, and in the middle a large dorsal fin gleamed proudly as it submerged and disappeared.

"Wow, Brah! That's too bad," said an unfamiliar voice.

"Who are you guys?" Mike asked turning to find three large Hawaiians also watching the aftermath.

"Makani sent you right?" asked Sam.

"Yeah, that's right. He wanted us to scare away this dude." He pointed to Wally "And the other...."

"Yeah, Brah, he's well taken care of," said the smaller Hawaiian.

Sam walked up to them and extended her hand.

"What? No. Ha?" exclaimed the Hawaiian.

"Yes, of course." Sam placed her forehead on each of them sharing the sacred ritual. "What are your names?"

Mike tried to extend the traditional greeting but was quickly refused, and his greeting was replaced with a simple hand shake.

"My name is Akoni, and this is Kaholo and Lono."

"I'm Mike and you obviously know Samantha." Mike felt like an idiot repeating her name.

Wally moved in and reintroduced himself in his Hawaiian name. "Wai'oli."

"Hey Brah, are you still working for that shark bait?"

"Hell, no Brah. I'm done with this bullshit."

"Good, what would your Akua think? Weren't there four guys?"

"Yeah, there were but Pono couldn't make it," said Akoni.

"Yeah...yeah I know."

"I definitely need a drink now," said Mike.

"Now you're talking Brah."

Sam looked out at the ocean covered in pink. Mike placed his arm around her.

"Looks like your prayers for protection have been answered."

Sam looked into his eyes.

"I didn't want them to be answered this way."

"Come on, let's get back to camp."

NINETEEN

THE PLANE TOUCHED DOWN at the Kahului Airport in Maui. Ramsay unfastened his seatbelt.

"Well here we are," said Ramsay.

Jerry stood up holding his briefcase. "Andrew!"

"Yes, Sir."

"Have you made all the arrangements?"

"Yes, everything has been taken care of —the car is waiting to take us to the hotel."

"Very good, Andrew. Ramsay, shall we?"

Ramsay grabbed his belongings and made his way to the exit. Once the door flew open, the humidity hit them like a sauna.

"Nice, isn't it?" Jerry asked as he followed Ramsay down the steps.

"Very, but it's a little overwhelming with the sudden shock of this high humidity."

"It is at that. I hope you brought the appropriate attire?"

"Not really."

"Well, that can be remedied. I'm sure the resort has

several apparel shops."

"Good."

Andrew held the door open as they entered the limousine.

"Thank goodness for the air conditioning," said Ramsay as he placed his belongings on the seat beside him.

"It is nice. Andrew, how long before we arrive?" asked Jerry

"It should be about forty-five minutes," confirmed Andrew.

"Very good."

The car exited the airport.

"Ramsay, have you ever been to the Hawaiian Islands?"

"What?" Ramsay was enjoying the view.

"Me? Oh no, never! It is beautiful, I will give it that."

"You can't see much in the dark. Wait till morning."

"I'm looking forward to it."

They drove down the road passing shops and residential areas until they reached an area called Wailea. Turning the corner, they noticed an impressive golf course.

"Look at that—what a great looking golf course!" declared Ramsay.

Jerry looked up from his papers. "Looks great, but need I remind you we're not here on vacation, this is business."

"I know, I didn't mean now—once business was done, of course," said Ramsay.

"Why is it that I feel like I'm scolding a child?"

"Really? What did I say to give you that impression?"

Jerry turned towards Ramsay and smiled. "Nothing just enjoying the scenery," he said, not wanting to get into what he really thought of him.

Ramsay was a partier, if there was a way for him to get out of his responsibilities and attend a night of drinking, he would. They were opposites when it came to their dedication to the service.

Although Jerry would occasionally attend the informal outings, he would refrain from the mischievous antics. Unlike Ramsay, who was an extremist partying hard and passing judgement without acknowledging the facts. The men that were under Ramsay's command didn't know what to make of him, and they would often keep their distance, saying as little as possible.

The men were also careful not to divulge any personal information for fear that Ramsay would use it against them once sober. Being intoxicated was his standard routine. Ramsay idolized him and any order that he presented to Ramsay, he would jump at, and that's exactly how he wanted it.

The limousine arrived at the front entrance of the opulent Fairmont Kea Lani Resort. They were greeted by the doorman and several eager bellmen who surrounded the limo in a synchronistic dance, opening doors and retrieving the luggage.

"Aloha and welcome to the Kea Lani,"greeted the doorman who presented Jerry with a drink and a traditional Hawaiian lei. Ramsay and Andrew were also greeted in the same manner by two rather striking looking women.

"This place is amazing!" exclaimed Ramsay.

The open air lobby was a marvel with its high vaulted ceilings and white marble flooring inlaid with an intricate circular mosaic pattern set at the center.

"Aloha and good evening." A sweet voice of a siren beckoned him to the front desk. "Aloha, my name is Jerry Alcott and we have reservations."

"Very good, Sir. Just give me a moment." Jerry turned to see Ramsay and Andrew exploring the lobby. A bellman had loaded their luggage on to a cart and was ready to transfer them to their rooms once he was given the room number.

"Sorry for the wait, Sir. I'll just be a minute."

"No problem."

"Stan, if you could please take their luggage to suites 396, 395 and 394."

Jerry could hear birds singing. When he looked around for the source he discovered that off to the side of the lobby there was a lovely atrium with bamboo trees for the birds to fly freely.

They followed the bellman down the long corridor. Jerry stopped to admire the most exquisite painting that he had ever seen. Its enormity was surpassed only by its sheer beauty.

The painting depicted the historic image of islanders curiously gazing out into the harbor at the approaching ships. Unaware of its significance that would forever change these islands. "Jerry! Are you coming?" shouted Ramsay.

"Coming."

The bellman led them to an elevator. Once they reached the third floor, the décor was the same lovely colors of tropical flora.

"Why thank you, Mahalo," smiled the bellman as Jerry tipped him generously.

"You're very welcome."

"Hey Jerry, meet you in the lounge in half an hour?"

"Why?"

"Well, we need to have a night cap."

"I suggest that you hurry; the lounge will be closing soon," said the bellman.

"Did you hear that Jerry? Hurry up."

Jerry picked up his luggage and walked into the bedroom. His bedroom had access to a balcony with a table and chairs. He was excited about the lounge where he could just lie back and enjoy the sun. The living area was separated with French doors, a large ceiling fan in the bedroom as well as the living room. An alcove came equipped with a coffee maker and a small fridge. He walked into the bathroom, which included a large bath, a wall to wall mirror, double sinks and a shower that resembled a grotto. His surroundings were definitely romantic, and for a moment he wished that he had someone to enjoy it with.

Although he welcomed his solitude, every now and again he wondered what his life would have been like if he had married and had a family. Oh, he had casual acquaintances throughout the years, but not that one special person.

He started to feel sorry for himself. Snap out of it, you are married to your career and that's all it will ever be, brutally echoed his voice of reason. Jerry decided to change his shirt into something more casual. Tonight, he will enjoy his surroundings, but tomorrow it will be all business.

TWENTY

"WHERE DID YOU GUYS camp?" asked Mike.

"Just on the other side of that bush," pointed Akoni.

"Oh well, that's not too far," said Mike.

"No, we can just stumble back." Akoni smiled.

"There you go. So, another beer? Wally, do you want one?"

"Yeah, OK."

Mike grabbed five beers and distributed them among the guys.

"Oh, Sam I'm sorry did you want beer or wine?"

"Glass of wine would be nice. Thank you Mike."

"We don't want to be drinking all your beers," commented Akoni.

Mike handed Sam her glass of wine.

"It's OK, we have plenty."

"Lono! Go and get some of our beers," ordered Akoni.

Lono stood up. "Kaholo you coming?"

"Ah Brah, can't you do it?"

"No! Come on you lazy."

Kaholo reluctantly got up. Akoni slapped him on the leg as he walked by.

"Nice guy, but lazy. If he can get away with doing nothing all day; that's when he's the happiest."

Mike broke out laughing. "I think if we all could get away with doing nothing, we'd be happy too."

"True. So what are you guys doing here?" asked Akoni.

Mike glanced at Sam.

"Well, we're looking for something," said Mike.

"Oh, could that something be on that ship?" asked Akoni.

"Hmm yeah, possibly."

Akoni shook his head. "That ship is hewa—wrong, bad."

Sam suddenly became interested and moved next to Akoni. "What do you mean, bad?" "There are stories—they say it's a ghost ship."

"What stories? Can you tell me more?" Sam was intrigued.

"They have said that storms will suddenly appear out of nowhere and lightning will strike the ship."

"Well, of course lighting would hit the ship—it's sitting in water and made of metal."

Akoni took a drink. "You find your reasons, but I am telling you when darkness falls in the light of day and the winds blow so hard that a person gets lost in its spiral; then there are no logical reasons to explain it away."

"That's weird Brah," said Wally.

"Hey guys, we brought the beer!"

Kaholo and Lono placed the beers in the cooler and grabbed a few to hand out.

"Good, Mahalo."

"Wally, what is weird?" asked Kaholo.

"Tom and I were parked in the brush back there, I left him for a while and when I came back to the truck he was gone."

"Gone? Really? Where did he go?" Sam asked.

"I don't know, but when I went out to look for him I found him face down on the ground."

Wally took a sip of beer.

"So what? He just fell," said Mike taking a drink.

"He might have, but it's what happened before he fell that was strange. He said that he left the truck and walked into the brush when all of a sudden the sky became dark and it was very windy."

"Hey Brah! Stop it! You're creeping me out," said Lono.

Akoni gave Lono a dirty look, and continued.

"It grew so dark that he couldn't see anything, and all he could do was hold his hands out in front of him to feel his way through the thick blades of grass. Next thing he knew he was face down on the ground."

"Strange, we didn't notice the weather changing, did we Sam?" asked Mike.

"No, actually it's been very clear."

"I know, right? It was. I tried telling him that, but

he insisted it wasn't. So anyway, I picked him up and we walked back to the truck He was acting pretty weird."

"Weird how?" Sam wanted all the details.

"He just sat in the truck not moving and looked off into the distance, as if in a trance."

"OK Brah, I'm serious. We're done with this shit!" Lono stood up."

"Sit down Brah, I'm not going to tell you again!"

"No, I don't want to hear anymore. I know it's what the locals call the feels and I definitely don't want to hear anymore," declared Lono.

"Stop being an idiot," said Akoni.

"You crazy, Brah, go get a beer," said Kaholo.

"The feels? What's that?" asked Mike.

"It's when you get a sense of something out of the ordinary that's about to happen," explained Sam.

"Did he eventually snap out of it?" Mike asked.

"Yeah, he did, but it was odd; it was like how can I describe it? He just didn't act like himself."

"OK, we're done." Kaholo stood up.

"Let's lighten up a bit. Anyone hungry?" asked Mike.

"Wally, are you?" asked Kaholo, hoping the question would stop him from telling his story.

Wally took a sip of his beer. "Yeah, I am."

"OK, then let's have something to eat. Sam are you hungry?"

"Sure."

"Need some help, Brah?" asked Kaholo.

"Yeah. You can help me with the propane. Burgers sound good, everyone?" asked Mike.

"It sure does," said Sam.

"Here let me help." Lono and Akoni stood up and joined Mike and Kaholo.

Sam moved in closer to Wally and whispered, "Did anything else happen?"

"Not really—oh, wait a minute. He was really hungry and mumbled something about the ship and that the key didn't unlock a treasure, but it unlocked something else. I asked him what, but he went quiet. I questioned him again, and he didn't know what I was talking about."

"That is strange. I was curious about the ship, but now this is becoming a whole new level of intrigue. When you guys came down to the beach, Tom was ranting about the treasure."

"Yes, he was his normal self, if you could call it that," said Wally. "You know I really don't like this place—it does give me the feels."

"I know there is a strange energy here, and I can't quite put my finger on it. Well, not yet anyway," said Sam.

"OK guys, dinner is almost ready, come and get your salads," called Mike.

"Wally, you go. I'll be right there." Sam walked down to the shore and stared at the ship, watching as the moonlight illuminated her ghostly hull.

She wondered why the ship did have a feel that was more than just a sea going vessel—a vessel that perhaps had an ulterior motive? Hopefully, it was nothing sinister.

"Sam! Come on, foods ready!" shouted Mike.

Sam rolled over in her sleeping bag. She heard distant voices, certain that she was dreaming until she heard her name being shouted. "SAM!" Come here! She unzipped her sleeping bag and threw on her shorts before leaving the tent. "What? What's the matter?"

The men had an unidentified man under restraint. "What's going on?" she walked up to Mike.

"Wally caught this guy sneaking around our camp," said Mike.

"Who is he?" asked Sam.

"We don't know. He won't say but he did ask for you—do you know him?" asked Wally.

Sam looked at the tall blond-haired man who was maybe a few years older than she was.

"No, I don't know him." At first glance he was definitely unrecognizable. She looked into his eyes and it was there that something seemed familiar, but she couldn't remember what.

"Well, we'll just take him into town," said Akoni.

"No wait!" shouted the stranger. "Samantha, you've found the box, right?"

"How did you know that?"

"Because……can he let go of me? I won't run away."

Mike looked at Wally and Akoni. "It's OK, let him go."

"Mahalo."

"So, you knew about the box, but how?" asked Sam.

"Because the box is mine," said the stranger.

"What! No, that's impossible!"

"Is it Sammy?" Sam turned in disbelief.

"No one has ever called me Sammy except my family. How did you know? What's your name?"

"It's Peter Underwood."

"OK Peter, quit playing around. Tell us the truth," said Mike.

"I am telling the truth. Sam look into my eyes."

"She's not going to look into your eyes you weirdo," cried Mike.

Sam walked closer to Peter. Wally grabbed hold of Peter's arm.

"It's OK Wally," said Sam.

"Sammy greet me in the traditional Hawaiian way and then everything will become clear," said Peter.

"No, Sam, that's too close." Mike stood in between Sam and Peter, bracing himself for a confrontation.

"It's all right Mike." Sam placed her forehead on Peter's forehead. For a moment there was nothing but the warmth of his forehead, then suddenly she was catapulted into her dream. She was in the hut. She couldn't see herself but could see the father giving the young boy a metal box. He explained what the box would contain and told them to lie on their beds. Sam obeyed, lying on her bed. Just as her dream had prophesied the surrounding mountains crumbled into the sea and destroyed their hut. Sam snapped back to reality.

"Sam are you OK? You're as white as a ghost," said Mike.

Sam slowly backed away from Peter, her eyes locked on his.

"This can't be—you're my brother and I'm your sister," she said softly.

Peter's eyes shone a brilliant blue. "Yes, you are Sammy."

"No, this can't be, but how?"

"Sam are you all right? What just happened?" Mike approached her gently touching her arm.

"Yes, Mike I'm fine."

"Here come and sit down." Mike guided her to a chair. Peter sat down beside her. Mike, highly protective, watched Peter's every move.

"How can I be your sister? That makes no sense."

"I knew you would find it hard to believe, but it's true," said Peter.

"But how can that be?"

"Well, our father worked for the government. He had developed a way to activate the ship, which was designed for communication purposes. To be more specific—finding life in our solar system. And in doing so, a means of travel through an unconventional way."

"He did that? That's phenomenal."

Sam couldn't believe what she was hearing.

"Now tell me why you think I'm your sister."

"Well, where do I start? You were born right here in Lanai."

"No, that's impossible. I was born in San Francisco."

"Look, Peter. Stop your charade you're scaring her," said Mike.

"I don't mean to, but she needs to know the truth."

"I just don't understand any of this."

"Sammy just listen. I'll start from the beginning."

"Please do."

"Well, a huge storm hit these islands, crushing our home and killing both of our parents. You were severely injured, and I had no means of taking care of you, so I carried you to a nearby farmhouse and left you at their doorstep. After knocking on the door, I hid in the bushes waiting until the occupants emerged. They were a young couple and I was certain that you would be well taken care of. I did check in on you by watching you play in the yard while I hid from sight."

"Well, thank you for being so concerned," said Sam sarcastically.

"I was—believe me. I hated to let you go. Sadly, they must have arranged for your adoption or moved to the States."

"I'd like to believe that Peter, but why didn't you come and get me if you knew I was all right?"

"I couldn't because there was no way that I could look after you. You looked so happy. I didn't want to complicate matters. Besides I needed to find the box; its contents were very valuable, and if they were ever found in the wrong hands it could have been dangerous. Father was really on to something big."

"Thank you for choosing the box over me, but as crazy as it sounds I can understand. So what do you mean about father?"

"Thank you Sammy I'm glad you understand. Father activated the ship with a special key that he forged from a meteorite. I have been searching for it ever since."

"Meteorite? Really!" exclaimed Sam.

"Yes, he discovered that no metal on Earth could produce the results that he needed."

"Interesting. What a genius!"

"Yes, he was. Do you see its importance now?" asked Peter.

Mike handed Sam a glass of wine. "I figured you'd need this right about now."

"Thank you, Mike, I sure do. Peter would you like a drink?"

"If it's no trouble?"

"No, trouble. Mike do you mind?"

"OK, I'll get it."

"Peter, I have something to tell you—I have the key."

"You do? Can I see it?" exclaimed Peter.

"Well you can, but I left it on the ship."

"On the ship? But why?"

"Let's say for safe keeping, someone was after it." Sam glanced over at Mike as he handed Peter his glass of wine.

"Someone was after it—who?" Peter took a sip of wine and was surprised by the robust flavor; since it was his first time indulging in alcohol. He now knew why people enjoyed it.

"What does all this information mean?" Mike asked.

"Our father created a direct opening to other universes," explained Peter.

"What? How? That's impossible."

"No, not impossible. It happened."

"And does the government know?" said Sam.

"Yes, they know, and they wanted to abort the project. So lucky for them the storm hit, and all was lost. But very unlucky for us."

"Then they obviously don't know you're alive." said Sam.

"Right."

"This is ridiculous!" declared Mike.

"Ridiculous as it may sound, it's the truth," said Peter.

Sam ignored their banter "So they assumed that the key and its secrets were forever lost, right?"

"Yes, until now," said Peter.

"Until now? What do you mean?"

"Sam, they know you're here."

"How?"

"He told them," said Peter glancing at Mike.

Mike stood up and backed off. "You're crazy! I didn't!"

"Oh, didn't you, well then why are they on Maui and ready to fly to Lanai once you contact them?"

"What! No that's impossible," shouted Mike.

"Why is that impossible Mike, tell us?" demanded Peter.

Mike was speechless.

"You did! Didn't you?" cried Sam.

"Listen to me! There's a logical explanation," begged Mike.

Sam slapped him across the face. "There's nothing logical about it. You fucking used me."

"Sam, I'll be honest. Yes I did in the beginning, but then I couldn't continue so I stopped communicating with them."

"Well, it doesn't matter what you did! They found us. Shit Mike! I trusted you. I can't believe it!"

Sam tried to compose herself, and Mike reached out to grab her, Wally quickly stood between them.

"No! Don't you touch me!" yelled Sam.

"Calm down," said Mike.

"Don't you tell me to calm down!" Sam began to pace, taking several deep breaths to calm herself down. "Let me get this straight. You are working with the government that is definitely a fact, but tell me what was Tom's part in this?"

"Tom, well you can say he drove me into taking the assignment."

"Drove you? Explain!"

"When the government approached me with an offer I had gambling debts, and I felt that there was no way out. I had no choice but to accept."

"I'm almost afraid to ask Mike. What was the offer?"

"I agreed that I would give them what they wanted, and what they wanted was you. I was to stay close and inform them of any unusual finds that you might have unearthed from your sites."

"What gave them the idea that I would find anything?"

"Well, they knew that you were the best in your field, and if and only if the box was to be recovered you would be the one to find it."

"So they weren't sure I would find it?"

"That's right, and believe me I was hoping you wouldn't."

"How does Tom fit into this?"

"Once the government paid me then I would pay him off."

"I am completely devastated. I can't believe you." Sam turned away to wipe the tears from her eyes.

"Sam please listen to me I was desperate, and the government offered to bail me out. I would have enough money left to start my life over. You have to believe me. I told them I found you and that's as far as it went; I never mentioned the box."

"You know what? I don't believe anything you say anymore."

"Please believe me. I'm telling the truth. When I last spoke to them, they had already known about the box. Someone else must have told them because it wasn't me."

"I don't care! Leave me alone. I don't believe a word you are saying," said Sam wiping her tears.

"Peter let's go. I need a walk." Peter followed Sam down the beach.

"Sam wait!" yelled Mike.

"Wow, Brah! Are you ever fucked! Come on, let's go guys," said Akoni.

"Wally, are you coming?" asked Akoni.

"No, I'm staying."

"Why?"

"Sam might need my help."

"OK Brah. Do you want us to stay?"

"No, I'll be all right."

"All right, Brah. Aloha."

Wally watched as they walked off into the brush, then he ran down to the beach following Sam and Peter.

TWENTY-ONE

"**H**EY JERRY! ARE YOU in there?" Jerry rolled over and placed the covers over his head.

Ramsay pounded on the door.

Jerry jumped out of bed annoyed. "What do you want?" He unlocked the door.

"Come on, let's go down for breakfast."

"I'm not even awake yet—you go."

"No, I'll wait for you."

Ramsay followed Jerry into the bedroom. "Hey, didn't we have fun last night?"

"What do you mean?"

"The three girls we meet at the lounge—remember?"

Jerry walked into the bathroom and splashed his face with cold water. "No. Refresh my memory."

"Yeah, you were pretty drunk. Well, we all were—even your man servant Andy." He laughed. "Anyway we were all sitting there minding our own business, when these girls walked down the stairs and asked if they could join us because the place was packed."

"I vaguely remember."

Ramsay laughed. "Well do you remember leaving with her?"

"What? No, I didn't."

"You sure did. If you don't believe me, ask Andrew he left with you guys."

"He did? Hmm—well then, I'm sure nothing happened. They most likely were leaving when we were, that's all."

"Well maybe, if you say so." Ramsay followed Jerry around as he changed.

"I was busy with a cute little number." Ramsay smiled.

Walking to the kitchenette, Jerry threw on his shorts and T shirt. "I need a coffee; do you want one? If I can figure out that machine."

"Ha, it's easy. Here, I'll do it." Ramsay made the coffee and walked out on to the balcony. "Here you go."

"Thanks." Jerry wasn't accustomed to a swirl of activity before having his morning coffee.

"Man, what a view! I could get used to this, that's for sure."

"Hmm, yeah not bad," said Jerry sipping his coffee.

"Not bad! You're kidding. Can you image waking up to this every morning?"

"Yes. It would be pretty nice."

"So, what's the plan for today?"

Jerry took another sip. "Well the plan is to go to Lanai."

"Come on Jerry, can't we spend one more day here?"

"Let me remind you that we're not on vacation; this is business."

"I know, but when was the last time you had a vacation?"

"A while."

"It's not like they're going anywhere. We know where they are, and we can rent a helicopter tomorrow."

Jerry hesitated, it did sound good. Business was business, but it had been a long time since he had a vacation. For once maybe Ramsay was right. "Man, Ramsay you're bad for business, but OK, just one day and then it's business as usual."

Ramsay slapped Jerry's leg. "Now that's my man—come on, let's go down for breakfast. I heard that their buffet is awesome."

"You did, hey? From whom I wonder."

"The girls, of course."

"OK. Enough about the girls, let's go."

They headed into the hallway where they were joined by Andrew.

"Hey guy, breakfast?" said Ramsay.

"Yes, Sir, I thought I would."

"Quit it with the Sirs, we're going casual—it's Ramsay and Jerry."

Andrew looked at Jerry who was rolling his eyes.

"Right, Sir, but—"

"Yes Andrew?" asked Jerry.

"But if you're Jerry, what is Ramsay's first name?

Ramsay jumped in. "Andy my boy, it's still Ramsay."

Ramsay pressed the elevator button.

Andrew wasn't content with Ramsay's answer. "Jerry what is Ramsay's first name?"

"Don't ask."

The elevator doors opened.

"Reminder. I do need to pick up a few items in their clothing shop this morning," said Ramsay as the elevator door closed.

Once the elevator reached its destination, Ramsay exited first. Jerry held Andrew's arm holding him back and whispered, "By the way Andrew, Ramsay's first name is Jedediah. That's why he goes by Ramsay."

"Oh. I see. Well, that is certainly an unusual name," said Andrew, stopping himself from smiling.

"What are you guys talking about?"

"Nothing just mentioning that the woman's voice in the elevator sound system sounded nice."

"She sure did. I'd like to meet her." Ramsay smiled.

"Ramsay settle down, will you? You would think you've never seen a woman before."

"Well, I really haven't seen so many beautiful women in one place, and hey, I'm just excited to be here."

"More ways than one," said Andrew.

Jerry glanced at Andrew. "You can voice your opinion anytime Andrew; it's not going on record."

"Right, Jerry."

"Here we are. Look at that pool!" Ramsay

wandered into the dining area.

"Yes, very nice."

"Can we have that table over there next to the railing?" asked Ramsay. "I want to have a view of the pool."

"Sure child," said Jerry.

"Aloha and good morning. Will that be for three?" asked the hostess.

"Good morning, and yes three for the buffet," said Jerry.

"OK, please follow me."

"Oh, can we sit there?" piped up Ramsay.

"Yes, you can, but let me have it cleared for you."

"Mahalo," said Jerry.

"This is perfect. Look we can jump right into the pool."

"Well don't do that," said Jerry.

"Later I will for sure. Well I'm starving. Let's see what they've got."

"You go ahead," said Jerry.

"Look out buffet here I come," said Ramsay.

They watched as Ramsay walked off into the buffet room.

"Andrew, once we're done can you try calling Mike. I want an update."

"Yes, Sir I will. Jerry, Sir, I'm confused."

"That's OK Andrew. Call me whatever makes you feel comfortable. Now let's go and see what they have to offer."

"Can I be quite frank with you?"

"What is it Andrew?"

"I really don't feel comfortable calling you by your first name."

"Really if it bothers you that much, then call me Talbot." Jerry smiled.

"Hmm, Talbot…yes…Talbot. That's better."

Jerry patted him on his back. "Come on, I'm starving—before Ramsay decides to devour everything."

"Guys, their selection is awesome!" Ramsay's plate was overflowing.

Jerry picked up a plate unsure where to start. Glancing over at Andrew who had no hesitations, Jerry wandered around eyeing the array of brightly colored fruits. He added some to his plate, and then he settled on an omelet made to order. Satisfied with his choices he returned to their table.

"That looks delicious!" said Ramsay.

"It sure does," confirmed Jerry.

"Once we're done eating, I'm going to buy a swimming suit and dive into that pool. It's definitely calling me."

"You know we really should leave and get to Lanai."

"Aw come on Jerry, you promised just one day and then we can go. I'll take whatever orders you give me."

Jerry glanced at Andrew, who was expressionless."

"Come on!" begged Ramsay.

"OK...OK. Just one day and then it's all business. We'll leave at first light."

"For sure! Thank you." Ramsay smiled. "Hey Jerry, look at that girl in the blue bikini."

Jerry looked over the railing. "She is very pretty."

"Maybe she's at the pool when I get there."

"Oh, I'm sure she will be."

Ramsay stood up. "Anyone getting more?"

"In a bit. Andrew, are you?"

"No, I'm done."

"You guys are lightweights." said Ramsay.

"Andrew if you're done, don't forget to try and get a hold of Mike."

"Yes, I'm going now."

"You don't need to go this very minute."

"No, it's OK. I'll go now." Andrew stood up and pushed his chair in.

"All right. Then I'll meet you at the pool."

"Right, Sir." Andrew turned to walk away.

"Andrew!"

He turned. "Yes?"

Jerry was about to correct him on his reply. He liked hearing Andrew say his name. He loved the British accent. "Nothing...see you later."

"Where did Andy go?" asked Ramsay.

"He had a few errands to run."

"Oh, I see, keeping him busy, are you?"

"You might say that."

"I can't get over this place—it's absolutely

beautiful. Did you know that they offer their guests a lot of fun activities?"

"No, I didn't know that, but I'm sure you'll engage in a few."

"You can bet on it. I was thinking about the Sunrise Outrigger one."

"That sounds interesting."

"You paddle out before sunrise and then back. Want to join me?"

"I don't know. Are you done yet?"

Ramsay nodded. "I am. I think my eyes are bigger than my stomach."

Ramsay pushed his plate forward and took a last sip of his coffee.

"Let's go then."

"So now, I'm going to do a little shopping. Care to join me?" asked Ramsay.

"I could use a few things."

"Good. I think that shop is actually—right here."

Ramsay walked into the boutique and straight into the men's wear.

"What do you think of this?" Ramsay held up a pair of brightly colored shorts in a flowered print."

"Definitely you."

"I thought so too. I'll just try these on."

"Go ahead."

Jerry wandered around and realized that he had forgotten to pack any sandals. He grabbed the shoes and a few other items and was finished in a few minutes.

Ramsay emerged from the dressing room. "How about this?"

"Looks great. Are we finished?"

"Yup, that's it. Care to grab a drink?"

"What? It's early."

"Something fruity and not too strong."

"OK. I'll play along."

"Good. Let's go."

They walked down the corridor and up the stairs into the lounge. "See there're guests here already."

"Let's find a seat—how about right there?" asked Ramsay.

They sat on a sofa facing lush tropical flora and the silvery shimmer on the ocean touched by the sun's golden rays.

"Morning, have you decided?" asked the waitress.

"Yes, I would like a Mai Tai," replied Ramsay.

"And I would like a Blue Hawaiian," said Jerry.

"Mahalo. I will be right back with your drinks."

"Mahalo. She's pretty."

"Ramsay will you stop commenting on every woman. It's a little annoying."

"Just making a comment. What's with you?"

The waitress returned with their drinks. "Mahalo."

"You're forgetting why we're here."

Ramsay took a sip. "I'm not. We're here to go to Lanai to put a stop to Samantha before she finds out what the government is up to."

"Ramsay shut up before someone hears you!"

"Sorry."

"In the morning we're out of here." Jerry was feeling a little guilty for taking the time off.

"But—"

"No buts. We're out of here or else I'm going without you. And don't you think I'll let you off easy. My comments on your conduct will be in my written report."

"Hey, no need to pull your weight around. We'll leave at first light."

"Good Ramsay. I'm glad that we understand each other."

Jerry quietly enjoyed his drink. For the first time Ramsay was silent.

"Will that be all, Makani?" Makani, who was looking away at the two men seated before him, turned toward the waitress.

"Yes, that will be all. Mahalo."

"Mahalo. I'm looking forward to your lecture this afternoon."

"I'm looking forward to seeing you there. Mahalo."

Makani stood up and glanced at the two men as he walked away.

TWENTY-TWO

"PETER TELL ME MORE. How did you know that Mike was a government agent?"

"I just knew. I've always known things since I was a kid. I could tell what a person would say before they said it—it's called telepathy."

"Telepathy. Did you always have this gift?"

"I remember having it as a kid, but it seemed to have become stronger once father activated the ship."

"That's interesting. Do you believe that the ship has something to do with it?"

"Possibly it enhanced my abilities. You know I'm certain that you possess the gift as well."

"What? Me? No, I don't think so."

"I believe you do; what do you call your dreams? It's your subconscious mind showing you the reality of who you really are. And our life together as a family."

"It's funny, but I can't remember a thing consciously."

"The mind is powerful and sometimes under extreme traumas it protects itself from harm by simply forgetting that an event ever occurred."

"I've heard of that—but for me possessing telepathy, I don't know."

"Have you ever tried?"

Sam smiled. "No, I haven't, and I'm not sure that I want to."

"Come on, let's give it a try," urged Peter.

"No. I don't want to."

"Come on try." Peter affectionately touched her arm.

"Well, all right then. What do I do?"

"Just face me and look into my eyes."

Sam turned facing Peter and looked into his eyes. "OK, now what?"

"Now clear your mind, and think of nothing."

Sam cleared her mind and looked into Peter's eyes. For a moment she saw blue flashes of light radiating from Peter's eyes, and then words started to appear in her mind. "You are wondering if we should go back or not."

"See you got it." Peter was impressed.

"Wow! Interesting—I can't believe it! I could never do that before."

"You've just never tried, that's all."

"Just a thought. Maybe it's because we're together and the connection is stronger."

"Hmm, could be very possible."

"So tell me more about our parents. I'm still finding it hard to believe that you are my brother."

"I knew it would be a bit of a shock, but I needed to tell you."

"A shock that's for sure, but how do you rewrite your life and delete the people that you grew to love?"

"Sammy you don't. No one is asking you to. Why do you feel that you have to surrender one way of life to accept another? You have grown that much richer as a person by expanding your love to those who have nurtured and loved you. There are no rules or limits to how and whom we should love—just love. You're very blessed to have two sets of parents who love you so very much."

"I never really looked at it that way—you are right. So tell me more. What were they like?"

"Here, let's sit down." Peter sat down on a log.

"Wally, I'm all right if you want to continue walking," said Sam.

"You sure?" asked Wally.

"I'm sure." Sam smiled.

"OK. I'll just be up the beach if you need me."

"Thanks Wally."

They watched Wally continue his walk up the beach until he found a spot to sit while still keeping an eye on them.

"Kind hearted guy and very protective of you."

"Yes, it seems that way, but it wasn't like that in the beginning."

"Well, I wouldn't judge him too harshly. Sometimes people make the wrong choices when they feel desperate. Instead they should just take a moment to step back from their situation and do nothing, absolutely nothing at all. Once their mind clears, they will receive the solutions to all their worries."

"I'm impressed with you brother. You are definitely making me think."

"Good."

"Now tell me with all this love talk, are you including Mike in the equation?" asked Sam.

"Well, maybe," smiled Peter.

"Honesty, I don't know if I can forgive him. What he's done to me far outweighs a parent and child relationship."

"All I can ask of you is to take it into consideration," said Peter.

"Noted. Anyway, tell me about our parents."

"Father was a genius you might say; he invented a device that under the proper conditions could rip a hole into parallel worlds and worlds beyond."

"Fascinating! How?"

"By using an electrical field that was so powerful and incorporating it with radio waves."

"Is that why he came to Lanai?"

"Yes, but he didn't know about the ship's capabilities at the time. It was only when he had found out that it was being used as a secret experimental vessel. Father had approached the government, who were at a stalemate until they heard of his theory. That's when they basically offered him anything he wanted, if he could make the project work. It was his dream and he was so excited. All he wanted in return was that his family accompany him, and the government agreed."

"Then how does the key come into play?" Sam was intrigued.

"Well he had the ship rigged up with the proper radio frequency, and the lightning storms supplied him with the electricity he needed. All he needed was a conductor to pull the two energies together."

"So what did he do?"

"He was becoming increasingly frustrated. Everything he tried failed. He was ready to abort the experiment when while walking on the beach to calm his frustrations, he noticed an odd shaped rock. Picking it up, he realized it was no ordinary rock, but a meteorite. So as a last-ditch effort, he decided to chisel a key out of it."

"Oh, I see and was he successful in activating it?"

"Well, he was about to put it to the test when the hurricane hit, and all was lost."

"And that's when you saved me."

"Right, and then I remained on this island in the hope of finding the box so that I could continue with father's experiment."

"Fascinating, but one thing I don't quite understand is how you became telepathic."

"As a child, I did have signs but only when a strange phenomenon happened. It was a bright sunny day until a windstorm seemed to come out of nowhere and the skies turned black as night, but just as quickly it mysteriously vanished. It was shortly after the anomaly we began to notice we could have conversations without speaking."

"Our parents as well?

"Yes, and you."

"This is strange" said Sam, "because Wally mentioned the same thing had happened to Tom."

"It happened again! And who is Tom?"

"Yes, apparently just the other day. Tom was a guy Wally was working for."

"Oh, and where is he? I'd like to speak to him."

"You can't. Unfortunately, he was attacked by a shark and killed."

"Poor fella."

"You can speak to Wally about it."

"I think I will, but what did he tell you?"

"Well, apparently it was a clear day that turned into a dark windy day out of nowhere. Tom had gotten lost and when Wally found him, he was acting strange."

"Do you know what this means?" exclaimed Peter.

"No, I don't."

"Let me ask you this, did you see anything strange?"

"No, the weather was a beautiful clear day."

"This is good!"

"Good? How can that be?"

"This means that they want to establish communication with us."

"They? Who are they?"

"I can't explain right now; but we have to get on that ship as soon as possible."

"It's getting late, so we can't go till morning."

"True. Then at first light."

"First thing in the morning. Now tell me more about telepathy."

"Father knew why we had developed telepathy, and when mother questioned him he explained that it was part of the second phase. And we should just enjoy our gift."

"Second phase of what?"

"Don't know, perhaps we'll find out once we complete father's mission."

"That's what I'm afraid of. Tell me what Mom was like?"

"Mom, well she was a very loving mother and wife. She believed in father's theory and supported him wholeheartedly, but she was fearful of his dealings with the government."

"Really? Why was that?"

"She felt that they were not telling him the whole truth, and that once father gave them what they wanted they could very easily get rid of us all."

"How did father feel about that?"

"He tried to reassure her that she was being far too suspicious, and he would just brush it off."

"What do you believe?"

"Unfortunately, I believed Mom. Father was far

too involved in his project to see the whole picture."

"So once the storm hit, I gather the government was happy that all was lost. It basically cleaned up all evidence of the project."

"True, but they never got what they really wanted."

"Let's finish what father started," said Sam. "Unfortunately, thanks to Mike we don't have much time."

"Yes, that's very unfortunate; we don't."

"OK then, tell me what to do and I'll follow."

"First things first. Let's get back to camp."

"Peter, just one question, would you have ever come looking for me if I didn't happen to show up?"

"Sammy, I knew you would show up." Peter smiled, nudging her arm.

"You're being a smart ass! But what if for whatever reason I didn't?"

"Sammy, I would have once I was certain that it was safe to do so."

"Peter, I'm glad to hear you say that," said Sam, giving him a shove that almost toppled him over.

"Hey, watch it! What was that for?" laughed Peter.

"Let's call it sisterly love. I have a lot of catching up to do in teasing my older brother."

"Ha! Oh do you now; don't forget that goes both ways."

Wally followed them back up to camp.

"Mike are you still here?" asked Sam.

"Yeah, you didn't expect me to leave, did you?"

"Well, actually I did."

"Sam, you're being crazy! You talk about trust—how can you trust this guy you've only known for what an hour?"

Sam grabbed three drinks from the cooler and handed Peter and Wally one.

"Well, I've known you for what the better part of my life, and look how you've deceived me."

"I don't know how many times I can apologize, but you're no angel either. You were quick to toss me aside when you felt that I was no longer of any use to you. So really you're no better."

"Mike, come on! We're talking about the government—you sold me out, this is big!"

"Sam, once and for all please listen to me! If it means anything, I stopped contacting them because I realized I couldn't go through with it."

"Mike, I really don't care."

"What can I do to make you forgive me?"

"Nothing! Don't you get it?"

"So, you want me to leave?"

"Yes, that would be the best idea you've ever come up with," said Sam.

"Fine. Then I'll leave, but there's one problem. I don't have transportation."

"So what? Walk!"

"Sam, come on."

"Sam we can take him into town in the morning," said Peter. "We have Wally to watch him for the night."

"Peter, I just want him gone."

"I know, but tomorrow."

Sam turned to Mike. "OK, tomorrow you're out of here and out of my life. Understood?"

"If that's what you want."

"That's what I want. Wally please watch him closely."

"I will. You can count on me."

"I think I need to lie down for a bit. I'm just exhausted with all this craziness." Sam walked over to her tent.

"Good idea, Sam! See you in the morning," called Peter.

"Early!" shouted Sam as she disappeared into her tent.

Peter walked up to Mike. "Can I have your cell phone?"

"What? I don't have a cell phone."

"I'm not going to ask you twice. I know you do. Give it to me."

Mike pulled out his phone. "Here but it's not charged; it hasn't been for a longtime."

"Good. Then you won't miss it." Peter threw it on the ground and stepped on it—crushing it. "Now that's better," muttered Peter as he disappeared into the brush.

"Fuck Man!" Mike grabbed another drink.

"You know, you could have taken Tom's truck," said Wally reaching for a drink.

"I know that, but don't you remind them, I need to stay," said Mike as he cracked a beer.

"Stay? Why?"

"Let's just say that we won't be alone for long."

"So they're coming?" asked Wally.

"You can be sure of that."

TWENTY-THREE

"**W**ELL I'M RUNNING UP to my room and dropping these off. Are you coming?" asked Ramsay.

"Yeah sure," said Jerry.

The waitress returned. "Will that be all?"

"Yes, we're good. Here let me sign for that." Jerry reached for his pen.

"Mahalo and have a nice day," said the waitress.

"Mahalo. Come on let's go."

"I can't get over this place," said Ramsay.

"You have mentioned it a few times."

"No, but really—look at that carving!" Ramsay ran up to an enormous craving of a mermaid with two large sea turtles. "She's beautiful—feel the smoothness of this wood."

"I admit it. Pretty nice." Jerry placed his hand over the carving.

"What I wouldn't give to have this in my home."

"Come on let's go. Where would you put it?"

"Oh, I'd find a place."

Jerry pressed the button for the elevator.

"So will I meet you down at the pool or do you want me to wait?" asked Ramsay as they entered the elevator.

"No, I'll meet you down there."

"Good," said Ramsay

The elevator stopped at their floor. They passed a maid who was busy cleaning out one of the rooms.

"Aloha," she smiled. Jerry reciprocated.

"See you in a bit," said Ramsay as he unlocked his room.

"Sure." Jerry entered his room, and closing the door behind him he noticed a note on the floor. What's this? He reached for the note, unfolded it, and read it out loud as he walked into the bedroom. "You don't know me, but I need to speak to you. Meet me in the smoking area in front of the hotel at one o'clock."

Jerry refolded the note throwing it on the dresser. He looked at his watch—twelve forty-five. He quickly changed his shirt and threw on his sandals. As he rushed out of the door he almost knocked Andrew over.

"Sir, oh excuse me."

"What is it Andrew? I'm in a hurry."

"I did what you asked, and I couldn't get a hold of him."

"Very good," said Jerry as he continued walking down the corridor.

"Do you want me to keep trying?"

"Yes sure, you do that. Now really, I'm in hurry."

Jerry ran down the hallway.

"Jerry!" yelled Ramsay.

Jerry ignored him.

"Andy, where's he going in such a hurry?" asked Ramsay.

"Sorry, but he didn't say."

"Oh strange. Anyway, are you going to the pool?"

"I wasn't thinking about it."

"Come on Andy old boy, have some fun! Here I'll wait for you while you get changed."

"You really don't have to you know," said Andrew nervously.

"I know, but come on hurry up, let's go!"

Jerry walked into the lobby; he wasn't sure where the designated smoking area was, so he asked the front desk. He was told to walk out of the front entrance and follow a path that would eventually break off into two. Following the instructions, he soon found himself in a hidden tropical oasis.

The dense foliage formed a canopy, hiding the occupants but not camouflaging the plume of smoke that floated throughout the air. He lowered his head as he entered, careful not to have his hair brushed by a massive leaf. There were several benches, one situated at the entrance and one that was hidden in the very back.

He chose the furthest bench which would give him a clear view of who entered. Looking around, he watched small green lizards hop from one leaf to the next. He was amused by their agility.

"Are you Jerry?"

"Yes, and who are you?"

"My name is Makani."

"I don't know you."

"No, you don't."

Makani sat down beside him. "I noticed you and your friends in the lounge, and I took it upon myself to find out your name and room number."

"And why would you go to all that trouble when you could have just introduced yourself?"

Makani felt he needed no explanation. "Do you know Samantha Woods?"

"Who? Sorry I don't," said Jerry.

"Oh, I think you do. Here let me refresh your memory. Sam is a well know archeologist here on the islands."

"Oh… well that's nice. As I said no, I haven't heard of her," said Jerry nervously.

"Come on now, stop playing games. You're definitely playing with the wrong person." "Games? I don't play games. As I said, I don't know her. So, if this is about her then I'm afraid we have nothing more to say." Jerry got up to leave.

"As you wish Jerry Talbot from Washington," said Makani.

He had Jerry's interest. Jerry sat back down.

Makani continued "And you are a general in the military and you—"

"OK, you have my attention. How do you know

all that? Did the front desk tell you?"

"No, do you want me to continue?"

"Go ahead."

"Mike is your undercover and you are here as a stop over until he signals you to travel to Lanai."

Jerry began to fidget. "How did you know?"

"How doesn't matter. What matters is that a dear friend of mine, Samantha Woods, is in danger and you are the root of it!"

"Look I'm not going to hurt her. I just want to stop her from finding out something that she shouldn't have ever been involved with," explained Jerry.

"Well, she's involved and I'm sure she'll have no trouble finding out what you're up to. By now I have a feeling that she already knows who Mike really is."

"I really hope that she doesn't. So let's get to the point shall we—what do you want?"

"Walk away," ordered Makani.

"You know I can't do that. What she's playing with is top secret."

"And obviously, being a government official, you will just make her go away if the secret is uncovered."

"Look if and only if it comes to that, you have my guarantee that I won't harm her."Makani stood up. "Guarantees—do you even know the meaning of the word?"

Jerry said nothing. Suddenly he felt very small and overshadowed by the large man.

"No, I didn't think so. Believe this Jerry Talbot. I

will do everything in my power to protect her. Do you understand?"

"I understand. Then we have nothing more to discuss."

"Nothing."

Makani walked out of the oasis not lowering his head. The canopy parted allowing him to walk freely.

Jerry waited until he was sure he was gone. How on earth did he know so much? Damn, he thought this assignment was going to be easy—just get rid of the people involved. Now it was getting complicated.

He searched for a cigar in his shirt pocket. He hardly smoked, saving them for rare occasions, and this was as rare as it comes.

An older man walked in smoking his cigar and noticed Jerry searching his pockets. "Forget your smokes?"

"Hmm, yeah I did. Changed my shirt and forgot to bring them."

"I know I hate it when that happens—here have one of mine."

The old man aided him in lighting his cigar.

"Thank you." Jerry took a long drag and exhaled. It did taste good.

"Do you mind if I sit here?"

"No, go ahead." Jerry moved over allowing the man to take a seat.

"So, where are you from?"

"Washington DC."

"Oh, that's quite a ways."

"It is a long flight. Where are you from?"

"Germany."

"Well, that's a lot further."

"It is at that. The wife wanted to come to Maui, and I wanted to go to the Maldives, since it was closer."

"Maldives. That would have been nice."

"It would have been, but you know how it goes what the wife wants she gets; otherwise she can make life hell for you." The old man chuckled.

"I wouldn't know."

"Not married hey?"

"No."

"Good for you."

"Is it? Sometimes I think it would be nice to have someone to share a life with."

"Ha! Share? Oh, no my boy. There's no sharing, but there is a lot of caring."

"Ah, is that the way it works?"

"Oh, by the way my name is Gunther Meyer."

"Jerry Talbot. Nice to meet you Gunther."

"So how long are you staying in Maui?" asked Jerry.

"We're here for seven days and you?"

"Actually, leaving first thing in the morning."

"Oh, that's too bad."

"It's really not a vacation; it's more for work, but next time it will be for a longer stay." Jerry finished his cigar, butting it out in the ashtray. "Well, it was really nice meeting you. Have a nice stay and thanks for the cigar."

"No problem, we might see you again before you go," said Gunther.

"You might, but if not, all the best."

"You too."

Jerry walked back into the lobby and made his way to his room. It was a quick change into his swim suit. He definitely felt like a swim and a drink, perhaps in reverse order.

TWENTY-FOUR

"**H**ERE GIVE ME YOUR hand." Peter reached down pulling Sam up through the ship's portal.

"Thank you, that was a lot easier than doing it myself."

"Yeah, a little helping hand certainly helps."

"Peter. I have a question?"

"Go ahead."

"Why is it that I have never noticed any sharks when we were in the water? I mean that was my deterrent every time I swam out here."

"Sammy. Sammy all you needed to do was to use your telepathy to tell them to back off." Peter smiled.

"Oh, brother really? I can't believe that would work."

"Well, my darling sister you believe what you will. I willed them to stay away and what did they do?"

"OK. I'm not going to question that. If that's what you did, and it worked—awesome! Come on, let's go; it's this way."

Peter followed Sam making their way topside.

"This ship is certainly in rough shape," observed Peter as he watched his step.

"Haven't you ever come aboard?"

"I did, but it's really deteriorated since then. Watch out!" yelled Peter.

Sam stopped almost stepping on a piece of jagged metal. "Thanks! I didn't see that coming."

"I don't want you to cut yourself on it—so where did you leave the key?"

"It's just over here."

Sam walked to the bow of the ship and opened the metal box.

"Here it is."

Peter carefully cradled the key in the palm of his hands.

"It's just like I remembered. Did you notice the markings on it?"

"Markings? No, where?" Sam leaned in for a closer look.

Peter cleaned the key on his shorts, and the dampness exposed the markings.

"Right here."

"Oh, there. Strange I didn't see it when I looked under the microscope."

"Did you wet it?"

"No, I didn't."

"Well there's your answer; it needed to be wet to be exposed."

"Hmm, learned something, so what do the markings mean?"

"Take a closer look, and you'll see the letter A then LOHA."

"That spells ALOHA."

"Right. Aloha, but why? What's its significance? Other than being a Hawaiian greeting?"

"Let's look at each letter individually. Now what if the letter A stands for alien, L for life, O for of and HA for breath in Hawaiian?"

"Yes, that's right."

"So let's piece it together—it could easily be read as Breath of Alien Life or Alien Life on Ha."

"But what is Ha?" asked Sam.

"In Egyptian times, there was a goddess by the name of Hathor. She was an Egyptian goddess who symbolized joy, music, dance and love, among other things."

"Peter this is incredible! Could that mean that the Hawaiian and Polynesian islands were home to aliens?"

"Possibly. Or the breath of alien life had touched all of Polynesia instilling the loving ways that all life on Earth should abide by."

"Whichever it may be, you can't deny that the traditional Hawaiian ways are unique and unfortunately not found all around the world," said Sam.

"True, and they do respect not just life as we know it but all life including plants, animals, mountains, rocks and the ocean. Did I cover everything?"

"I think you did." Sam smiled. "It's sad that the majority of the world doesn't live by that code."

"Yes. I wonder if alien life had populated the islands with an intent on teaching us a beautiful peaceful way to live together as one. Could that be the magic we feel once we visit these islands?"

"It's quite possible; however, I believe that not all the people that visit react in the same way. I'm sure only a select few. It would be an interesting hypothesis if alien life were the first inhabitants."

"It certainly would," agreed Peter.

"I wonder if we're going to find any answers to our questions."

"Let's continue looking and see what answers we find. Sam did you see anything on the ship that looked like a radio transmitter?"

"No, I didn't."

"I'm sure it's got to be here somewhere."

"Right. Peter you lead. Are you going to leave the key?"

"No, I'll bring it. You hold on to it. I don't think it belongs in that box."

Sam placed the key in her top for safe keeping.

"Where do you think it belongs?"

"I'm not sure. Let's look around."

"Peter, I just remembered another strange thing about the word ALOHA. Apparently the origins of the word are unclear."

"Really? It would be great if we could find out."

"Definitely!" confirmed Sam.

"Did you look at the stern?" asked Peter.

"No, I didn't."

Sam followed Peter. "Do you really think it might be here?"

"Not sure, but worth checking out."

"Ouch!"

"Sam are you all right?"

"I am. Stupid thing tripped me."

"Here, let me check your leg."

"I'm OK. It's that stupid piece of metal, it almost killed me."

Peter pushed away the metal debris to further expose a large metal door. Sam rubbed her ankle.

"Sam you found something!"

"I did?"

"Look! It's a door!"

"Here let me help you."

Peter pulled on the ringed handle and with Sam's help exposed an opening into the center of the ship.

"I wonder where it goes."

"Only one way to find out."

"It's pretty dark down there—we should have brought a flashlight," said Sam.

Peter looked up in the sky to determine whether the sun's angle would help light the chamber.

"You know we should be OK—the sun's angle is in perfect alignment to give us light."

Sam glanced up, shielding her eyes. "You're

right—hopefully that works."

Peter grabbed on to the edge and lowered himself into the hole. Finding his footing on a ladder, he grabbed Sam's waist as she carefully lowered herself down. Reaching the bottom, they began searching for something that would resemble a transmitter.

"Peter it's still dark in here. I can hardly see."

"Just give it a moment for your eyes to adjust."

The sun's rays were directly shinning down into the dark room, exposing a large metal table with several tiers.

"What's this?"

"Peter did you find something?"

"Look!"

Sam slowly walked over, careful not to bump into anything.

"It looks like a large podium. What's this on it? Plexiglass?"

Sam placed her fingers along the edges of the podium.

"Looks like it."

"Sam what are you doing?"

"Checking for any hidden devices."

Peter examined the base of the wooden pillar.

"Interesting."

"What? Did you find something?"

"You tell me. What does that look like?"

Sam bent down for a closer look.

"It looks like an imprint of a key. Here look."

"It does! It really does."

"Here give me the key."

Sam reached into her top and handed Peter the key, who then placed the key on to the imprint and stood back, anticipating an immediate reaction.

"Nothing's happening," said Sam.

"Yeah. I guess we keep on looking."

Peter was disappointed. He was certain that they had found what they were looking for.

"Man, I thought that was it for sure," Sam said.

"Me too." Peter left the key in its spot and they continued to search.

"Here, maybe there's something in this table," said Sam.

They opened the drawers only to find nothing.

"Peter!"

"Yeah. What?"

"Doesn't it seem like the room is getting brighter?"

Peter looked up from his search. "You're absolutely right, but where is it coming from?"

"Peter look!" Sam pointed to the podium, which was now lit in a blue glow. They cautiously approached the source of the light. The Plexiglass had lit up and was now displaying an image of the solar system.

"This is incredible—look at all the planets!"

"They're rotating; how can that be? There's nothing mechanical that could cause it to move."

Peter searched the pillar for the source of the movement.

"I know—this is very strange. Look isn't that Mars? It's so close to the Earth, and what is that? Are you seeing what I'm seeing?"

"I do, but I can't believe it!"

Peter and Sam were mesmerized by the radiance of the colors. They watched as a red ring formed around the Earth and then slowly dissipated only to be replaced by a blue ring and finally ending in gold.

"I wonder what that meant?" asked Sam.

"I really don't know. I have no idea."

As suddenly as the display had come to life, it was now dark and motionless.

"Well that was something!"

"That reminds me when I found the key, I did find a map with the solar system on it minus the rings."

"You did?"

"Yes, I was so focused on the key that I wasn't sure about its significance at the time, but now it obviously is a part of the puzzle."

"I'd like to take a look at it when we get back."

"For sure."

"Come on, let's go."

Peter was the first to climb up the ladder when suddenly the metal door slammed shut and surrounded them in darkness.

"Peter? Peter? Are you OK?"

A moment of silence engulfed the compartment.

"Peter!" screamed Sam.

"I'm fine," whispered Peter.

"Where are you?"

Peter stretched out his arms, searching for her. "I got you."

"Peter, what are we going to do?"

"I'll see if I can open the hatch. Here, hold on to me."

Peter placed Sam's hand on his leg as he ascended the ladder. He reached for the hatch and placed both hands on the cold metal.

"Sam are you still there?"

"I'm here."

"Good, don't let go."

Peter pushed on the hatch, which was proving to be futile. It was far too heavy. He gave it one last try, leaning his body into the ladder for support and one final push. It moved a little but not enough to open it.

"Sam! I don't think I can open it—it's far too heavy."

"Shit Peter! Now what?"

"I'm coming down. Watch yourself."

Sam felt Peter's body sliding past hers.

"We have to find another way out. Here hold on to my arm."

Sam held on tightly.

"Hopefully we can find another way out. Do you really think there is one, or should we try the hatch again?"

"No, it's just way too heavy."

"Peter look! Isn't that a light?"

"You're right! Come on."

They carefully inched their way towards the light.

"Could it be a door?" said Sam.

"Not sure."

Peter searched for an opening along its surface. Finding a groove along the edges, he gently pulled and exposed an entrance.

"Sam here give me your hand."

Sam positioned her fingers next to his.

"Here. On the count of three, help me pull."

"OK."

"One, two, three, pull!"

They pulled in unison until the door opened with just enough space to exit. A flood of light poured in along with an enormous amount of water.

"Come on hurry, there's the porthole," yelled Peter.

Sam grabbed on to Peter's arm as they rushed into the compartment that was now quickly filling up with water. They held their breaths as they were being completely submerged and swam towards a large opening that proved to be the porthole.

Their bodies were being pushed back into the chamber as they fought the rush of incoming water. With the danger of running out of air they managed to fight its force by being pulled through the porthole and deposited into the sea.

Sam was the first to surface. "Peter! Peter! Where are you?"

Peter surfaced within inches of Sam. "I'm right here!"

"Peter, we forgot the key!"

"Never mind. Let's get back to shore."

Wally watched from camp as Peter and Sam battled the waves. Once they had reached the shore, he ran down to make sure that they were all right. Mike followed.

"Are you OK?" Wally was looking down at Sam who was trying to catch her breath. "Yeah, I'm fine," said Sam, coughing up sea water. "Where's Peter?"

Wally looked up and down the beach. Mike was bending over Peter. "He's fine, Mike's with him."

"No!" Sam jumped up and ran towards Mike.

"You leave him alone!" yelled Sam.

"He's fine I just wanted to help him up," said Mike.

"Get away from him!"

"Sam you're crazy if you think I'd harm him."

Sam wrapped her arms around Peter's waist pulling him up to his feet. "Just leave him alone! Get out of my way!"

Mike backed off.

"Are you OK?" asked Sam.

"I'm all right," confirmed Peter.

Sam placed her arm around Peter as they walked back to camp.

"Here you go." Mike held out two towels."

Sam ripped the towels out of his hands and

wrapped it around herself and Peter.

"Peter here sit down beside me."

"Well, if it means anything, I'm glad that you're both safe. Did you happen to find anything?"

"It's none of your business if we did."

"Come on, give it up Samantha."

"Give what up? Just go away."

Mike looked into Sam's eyes for a glimpse of sympathy, but there was none.

"OK fine, I'm going for a walk. When I come back I hope you can at least treat me with an ounce of kindness given the history we once had."

Sam and Peter watched as Mike walked up the beach.

"I can't believe him."

"You know Sam, he might have a point."

"What! Don't tell me you're taking his side! You know what he did—he used me!"

"I know, but maybe just back off a bit. I'm not telling you to forgive him—just be civil."

"Peter, I don't understand you."

"You don't have to, but I hope you understand the word compassion, do you?"

"Oh Peter that hurts. Are you accusing me of not being compassionate?"

Peter stared at her in the hope of finding a trace of that attribute.

"Well, fine. I'll give it a try."

"Good. That's my Sammy. Now, you know what?

I'm hungry. Anyone else?"

"I'm feeling it. That was quite the swim—I've never seen the waves that big since we've been here."

"I know they were huge. I didn't think you guys were going to make it," added Wally.

"Honestly, we didn't think so either," said Peter.

"Here, let me fix us something."

"Wally, don't tell me you cook?" said Sam.

"I try. My wife says I'm a pretty good cook."

"Well, if your wife says you are, then Wally be our guest."

Wally smiled. "OK, I'll get started."

Sam ran into her tent."

"Where are you go—?"

Before Peter could finish his sentence, Sam was back and unraveled a piece of paper. "Here, this is what I found with the key."

Peter examined the diagram of the planets. "Interesting, look at this."

Sam leaned in. "What?"

"I don't see the rings around Earth," said Peter.

"Hmm…I wonder why not. We saw it on the Plexiglass."

"Maybe this map was created prior to the image we saw on the ship," suggested Peter

"Could be. What do you make of it?"

"I really don't know. But if you notice Mars is situated very close to the Earth just as the image on the ship had depicted."

"You know, you're right. What do you think this means?"

"Not sure, but I have heard of times when Mars was very close to our Earth just like the moon. But this close is rare," said Peter.

"From Earth's perspective, it would look like Mars were our Moon. What a sight that would have been! Two planets in our night sky."

Peter nodded.

Sam noticed Mike returning. "Oh, let's stop talking about this. Mike's back."

"Now remember Sam," warned Peter.

"Yeah, all right. Mike would you like a drink?" asked Sam.

Mike was taken aback as Sam stood by the cooler.

"You talking to me?" Mike looked around to see if anyone else was there.

Sam glanced at Peter for approval. He smiled.

"Yes, I'm talking to you. Do you want a drink?" Sam knelt down and pulled out a bottle of wine. "Is red OK?"

"Sure fine."

Mike sat down beside Peter. "So, what is Sam up to?"

"What do you mean?"

"She's being nice to me."

"Maybe she had a change of heart."

"Sam—not the Sam I know."

"Well, Mike just go along with it, if you know what's good for you."

"OK, no questions," said Mike.

"Here you go." Sam handed the men their glasses of wine.

"Sam do you want to sit down?" Mike stood up.

"Oh, no. Thanks. I'll just sit here on the other side of Peter. Cheers!"

Mike waited until they all took a drink before having his.

"This is great wine!" exclaimed Peter.

"I take it you're not a big drinker?" said Mike.

"No, not at all. Neither were my parents."

"Really? Didn't they drink?" asked Sam.

"Well, occasionally father would but Mom never touched the stuff."

"I still can't believe you're brother and sister," said Mike.

"I suppose it would be rather hard to believe. Especially when you met her parents and basically grew up together."

"Yeah. It's hard to wrap my head around it. So don't take offence if I keep my guard up."

"Absolutely, no offence taken. I wouldn't want you to do anything less. After all you do care a great deal for her, don't you?"

Mike paused deciding whether to answer his question. Taking a good long drink, he looked over at Sam who was busy helping Wally.

"I care for her more than she'll ever know."

"That's what I thought," said Peter.

TWENTY-FIVE

"**Y**OU MADE IT!" said Ramsay.

"Yes, I did. Where did you get the towels?" asked Jerry.

"Just over there—by the grey bins."

"Oh, where the guys are standing?"

"Yup, and there's sunscreen and water by the pool."

"OK, I'll be right back." Jerry picked up some sunscreen and two white towels and returned to the lounge. He unraveled the towels and placed them on his chair making himself comfortable.

"All set?" asked Ramsay.

"I think so. This is nice."

The waitress came by. "Can I get you something to drink?"

"I'll have a Blue Hawaiian," said Jerry.

"And you?"

"Mai Tai."

"Can I have your room numbers?"

They gave their room numbers.

"Mahalo."

"So where did you go in such a hurry?" asked Ramsay.

Jerry adjusted his chair. "What?"

"When I saw you earlier you rushed right past me."

"Oh, just had to ask the front desk something."

"Is that all? I thought it might have been business."

"No, nothing to do with that."

"Good. You promised business was to be canceled for today."

"I can't believe how you talked me into staying here and relaxing when we have important business to do," complained Jerry.

"Yeah, well it didn't take much convincing. Maybe a part of you felt like you needed a vacation."

"Maybe."

The waitress returned with their drinks. "Here you go. Can you sign for this?" The waitress handed Jerry the note and pen. "Mahalo."

"Mahalo."

"Here Jerry." Ramsay held out his glass. "Cheers! I can't believe how good this is. How's your Blue Hawaiian?"

"Very good."

"Oh, look, they have a hammock."

Jerry looked at two palm trees that were anchors for the swing.

"It looks comfortable, if you can manage to get into it. I'll give it a try later."

Jerry lay back enjoying the warmth of the sun. He was starting to feel guilty, since he was never one to remain idle. Placing his work first and foremost felt more like his comfort zone. Now Ramsay, on the other hand, was the opposite.

Relaxation and play were his priority. Ramsay's work ethics when in full dedication were relentless. He was nicknamed the bulldog, which proved to be borderline psychopath. Maybe a little relaxation was a good idea; he needed all his strength to contain the bulldog.

Jerry leaned over and grabbed his drink from the side table. His mind wandered to the strange meeting he had earlier. Who was this guy that seemed to know everything? Perhaps Mike had filled him in on the details. Yeah, that was it—he was sure of it. The heat was starting to get to him.

"Geez, it's hot out here. I'm going for a swim."

"Yeah, go. I might join you in a bit."

Jerry walked past several lounge chairs adorned with sun-soaked bodies before entering the pool. The coolness of the water rushed over him as he slowly entered. Deciding it was best to brave the sudden cold shock, he submerged himself and immediately swam to one end of the pool.

Once he surfaced, he held on to the side of the pool, impressed by swimming the length in one breath. As he looked around the pool, he noticed that most of the people were couples. For a moment he felt like the loneliest man in the world until he spotted several women who were laughing among themselves—enjoying a girl's trip perhaps. To his surprise there seemed to be a lot of men who were very much on their own. He now felt like the majority. He watched as the waitresses walked into an outdoor restaurant to have their drink orders filled. The bartenders created the most elaborately stunning drinks he had ever seen. The bar was also a restaurant called Kō. I'll have to check out the menu, he thought to himself. He was about to swim back when he felt his legs being pulled.

"Hey!"

Ramsay surfaced laughing.

"What the hell are you doing?"

"Just letting you know I'm here!"

"You're crazy!"

"Aw, I'm loving this. Hey, what's that—a restaurant?"

"Yeah, it's called Kō. I was just thinking we should try it tonight."

"I'm game. By the way, where's Andy?" asked Ramsay floating on his back.

"I don't see him. Maybe he changed his mind."

"Yeah, maybe. Well anyway, race you back."

Ramsay pushed off gaining an advantage over Jerry.

Jerry gained speed over Ramsay leaving him behind. Surfacing at the opposite end of the pool, he jumped out and walked back to the lounge.

Ramsay returned. "Pretty good, you beat me, but it wasn't a fair race you know."

"Ramsay, you could never stand losing."

Jerry adjusted his towel and lay down. He enjoyed the coolness of the pool, which made the heat tolerable.

The waitress returned. "Would you like another drink?"

"Sure, the same, Ramsay?"

Ramsay looked over. "OK, the same."

Jerry and Ramsay watched as the waitress walked off, placing other orders. They both happened to turn and look at each other.

"What?" smiled Jerry. "Yes, she's attractive."

They sat in silence. Ramsay lay on his stomach and checked out the lovelies in front of him. A beautiful young blond-haired girl with the cutest figure was trying to take a selfie of herself. She was positioning her locks in the most flattering way to create her prefect pose.

Was she alone, Ramsay wondered? No sooner than his thoughts left his mind, he received his answer. A man came rushing up to her, ranting about something that had obviously upset him. Ramsay couldn't make out what was being said. The woman tried to calm him down, but he continued ranting as they packed up and walked past Jerry.

"Hey Jerry!"

"What?"

"Did you see that guy?"

"What guy?" muttered Jerry.

"He looks familiar."

"So?"

"No really. I think he's a celebrity."

"Yeah, well I'm sure they have several who stay here."

"Will you look?" Jerry opened his eyes, shielding them from the sun.

"Who?"

"Those two over there—wait till he turns around. That guy, isn't he from a band?"

"Maybe." Jerry took advantage of being disturbed and took a drink.

"I'm sure he is, but I can't place him. Damn I hate that when you can't remember. I know it's going to bug me all day until I get it."

"Ramsay, who cares? Let it go."

"Man, he was pissed about something. Isn't he Irish?"

"Ramsay, I really don't know, and I don't care."

"Yeah, I think he is. Man, does he have a temper."

Jerry stood up.

"Where are you going?"

"I'm going for a smoke."

"I didn't know you smoked."

"On occasion and this one because you're driving me crazy."

Jerry walked down an embankment which lead to an oasis for smokers. Sitting on the bench, he lit his cigarette, enjoying his moment away from Ramsay.

"Hello again."

Jerry turned around to see a couple joining him.

"Oh hello. Gunther Meyer is it?"

"Yes, that's right. We met earlier."

"Yes, I remember."

"This is my wife, Luisa."

"Hi Luisa, nice to meet you. I'm Jerry."

Luisa smiled and pulled out a cigarette, and her husband assisted in lighting it.

"Are you liking your stay, Luisa?"

"Yes, very much. Where are you from?"

"Jerry is from Washington DC," replied Gunther.

"Oh, is that a long flight?"

"Yes, but not as long as yours."

Luisa smiled.

"Have you seen much of the island?" asked Jerry.

"Actually, we have reserved a helicopter tomorrow morning at six so we can have an aerial view of the islands," said Gunther.

"Fantastic!"

"Yes, but Luisa is not sure if she wants to go."

"Why is that?" asked Jerry.

"I've never been in a helicopter, and I'm afraid I might get motion sickness."

"Oh that's not good, but I'm sure you'll be fine. Try taking a motion sickness pill; it should help."

"Where can I get some?"

"I'm sure the hotel supplies them."

"Gunther, we'll have to get some."

"Yes dear, we will. Thank you, Jerry."

"No problem." Jerry finished his cigarette. Well, nice meeting you Luisa and I'm sure we'll see you again. If not, enjoy your trip."

"Yes, you too Jerry." Luisa smiled.

Jerry returned to his lounge to find that Ramsay was no longer there. Most likely he went for a swim, which was good, since he was fed up with Ramsay's gibberish. He closed his eyes and was about to doze off when he felt a shadow over him. Opening his eyes, Andrew stood before him.

"Hi, Andrew. I see that you've decided to join us."

"Sir, I thought a little refreshing dip would be nice."

"Absolutely! I want you to enjoy yourself. You deserve it. I'm so glad you decided to join us. Ramsay is driving me crazy."

"He does seem to have that effect on people."

Andrew organized his towel and then wandered off to the pool.

Again, Jerry closed his eyes. A slight wind had picked up, which was refreshing. He tried to recall when he had last vacationed, but nothing surfaced. It wasn't something that he did. Co-workers would often brag about their exotic getaways, but he couldn't relate. Well, at least now he could honestly understand its importance in clearing the human psyche.

"Jerry! Jerry!"

Great, he was back. "Yeah Ramsay what?"

"I checked out this neat little bar, it's called Ama."

"That's nice."

"You have to walk up the stairs. It's just past the kid's pool."

"Great," said Jerry as he took a drink.

"It's just over there—do you see it?"

Jerry looked in the general direction and noticed a tall building with several stairs leading up to a bar.

"Did you try the food?"

"No, but I did look at the menu and everything looked great. I thought we could grab something in a bit."

"Well, we can go there, or do you want to go to Kō?" asked Jerry.

"What's Kō?"

"The restaurant at the end of the pool."

Ramsay glanced over. "It doesn't matter to me, but Kō looks more like a fancy dinner place. Why don't we have dinner there and a couple of appetizers at Ama? Best of both worlds," smiled Ramsay.

"OK, why don't we do that?"

Andrew returned from his swim.

"Andy! How was your swim?" asked Ramsay.

"It was very refreshing." Andrew arranged his towel on the lounger and lay down.

"Would you like a drink, Andy?" asked Ramsay.

"I don't mind if I do."

"That's my good man. What would you like?"

Andrew looked over at Jerry's drink. "What are you having?"

"A Blue Hawaiian—it's made with rum, pineapple juice and some blue stuff," explained Jerry, flagging the waitress.

"Hmm, that does look rather yummy. I do believe I'll have one."

TWENTY-SIX

"**W**ALLY THIS IS REALLY good," said Sam, taking another mouthful.

"I'm glad you like it—it's my own creation of ground pork, tomato sauce, onions and garlic over rice."

"It's really tasty, isn't it Peter?"

"Absolutely! It beats anything I've eaten."

"What did you eat? I mean did you go into town at all, or just basically hide out in the bushes," asked Mike.

"Mike!" snapped Sam.

"What? It's a legitimate question."

"It's OK Sam, I'll answer it. I did a lot of fishing and there were generous people who invited me into their homes for meals."

"Does that answer your question?" asked Sam.

"It does, but I see nothing wrong with my asking."

"What! Did you assume he was a wild man pillaging for his food?"

Peter intervened before Mike could respond.

"Sam, it's OK. I answered his question."

Sam shifted her attention to Wally. "So Wally can you tell me the history or are there any legends of Lanai?"

"Yes, there are legends. This island is considered haunted with evil spirts."

"Evil spirits? Really? Tell us." Sam took a drink of her wine.

"A son of the Maui chief exorcised this island. Some say that an orange glow of fire could be seen from Maui. Some still believe it's haunted with ghosts of the Night Marchers. The

Night Marchers are the ghosts of warriors. They are considered to be deadly. And if one were to cross their path, they should lie on the ground face down, to show a sign of respect. And in doing so you might be spared."

"Yes, that's right Sam," said Peter. They continue to march, ready for battle for all eternity."

"That gives me the shivers," said Sam. "Now changing the subject Wally, I vaguely remember that Makani mentioned something about petroglyphs?"

"Yes, actually they're not too far from here."

"Really?" Sam looked at Peter. "Can you show us?"

"I sure can. Do you want to go now?" asked Wally.

"Can we? We still have a couple of hours before the sun sets."

Sam stood up ready to leave.

"OK then, let's go." Wally started to walk up the beach.

"Can I come?" asked Mike. Sam ignored him.

"Yeah, come on," motioned Peter.

They walked up the beach until they reached a large boulder with the inscription of Shipwreck Beach, turned right and then followed the signs. It was a bit of an uphill climb along sharp lava rocks, which made for a slow trek.

"Why didn't we drive?" asked Mike, almost slipping on a jagged boulder.

"We can use the exercise—besides it's not that far," said Peter.

They walked through the brush until they came to a clearing.

"There look!" indicated Wally.

Peter ran up to the first petroglyph he found. Sam followed. "That's interesting, look at the shape of the man," she said.

Sam knelt down for a closer look. "The shape looks much like a human, but the head resembles that of a bird."

Peter bent over for a closer look. "You know, you're right, it does."

"Hey, look at this!" yelled Mike. "There's a few more of the humanoid shapes."

Peter and Sam joined Mike.

"Interesting, and here doesn't that look like a space ship?" asked Wally.

"You know it really does. This is incredible," said Sam as she rubbed off some of the dirt on the drawing.

"I'm glad you're enjoying this, Sam," replied Wally.

"I definitely am," beamed Sam.

"Come on, let's start heading back," urged Peter.

"You know Sam," said Wally walking alongside Sam, "There are many sites to be seen on this island. In fact we have a garden called Garden of the Gods."

"I have heard of the garden."

"You have?"

"Yes, isn't it said that the stones were fashioned by the gods because of their love of art and that they used strong winds to create them."

"That's right. Lanai is a just a treasure trove of legends."

"It is a very beautiful island; every beauty does have its mysteries. Wally, you know that feeling of déjà vu that strange feeling of being somewhere before—well I felt it as we walked around the petroglyphs."

"That is strange. Were we all included in your déjà vu?"

"Yes, everyone's actions and reactions."

"I wonder why you felt like that."

"I really don't know."

"Hey, wait up!" shouted Mike who had fallen behind.

"Well, hurry up!" called Sam.

They stopped and waited for him to catch up.

"OK, Wally, lead the way."

They walked single file down the hill.

"Careful Sam, watch your step," cautioned Peter.

"I will."

Peter was being every bit the protective big brother and she loved it. They made good time descending and soon they were back at camp.

"Mahalo Wally for showing us the site—it was very interesting," said Peter.

"You're very welcome. I thought you might enjoy it."

"Anyone thirsty?" asked Mike. "I wouldn't mind something to drink."

"I think that goes for all of us Mike."

Mike pulled out bottles of water.

"What water?" exclaimed Sam.

"OK, Mike, are you possessed or something? Water?" laughed Peter.

"I thought water would be a good start." Mike smiled.

"I would like water, Mike." said Wally.

"Thank you, Wally, for seeing it my way."

Mike picked up a water bottle and handed it to him. Peter stood up and picked out a bottle of wine and gave Sam a cup and poured.

"Well, you guys enjoy your water; we'll have our wine."

"Go ahead. You know, I'm feeling pretty tired. I think I'll call it a night," said Mike.

"What already?" said Peter.

"It's been a long day." Mike walked over to his tent.

"Well, OK, night." Peter elbowed Sam in the arm.

"Yeah, night. What's up with him?"

"Don't know, but maybe it's your attitude."

"My attitude? Don't get me started."

"Why would I want to do that? I know you'd never shut up," said Peter and laughed.

"Gee thanks. Love you too, my brother." Sam took a sip of wine.

"Peter tell me where did you camp?"

"Well, it's not very far—just up the road a bit and in the brush."

"Oh. Well, don't count on going back there tonight. You're staying here."

"No."

"I insist." Sam was beginning to feel the effects of the wine, playfully hitting Peter in the arm. "Aw come on."

"All right. I'll stay, but just let me run up and grab my sleeping bag."

"I'll come with you." Wally looked over at Sam. "Do you want me to stay?"

Sam hesitated, looking over at Mike's tent. "No, I'll be fine, you go."

"Be right back," said Wally.

Sam watched as they disappeared over the embankment and into the brush. She leaned back in her chair staring at the night sky. The Milky Way stretched in an arch over her head and over the ghostly ship.

There was something about the Milky Way that was so celestial. Looking around the vast sky she noticed that Mars was unusually close to Earth. She wondered why.

"So, are we OK?" Sam jumped out of her seat.

"Mike, my god you scared me."

"Sorry, I didn't mean to." Sam could feel her heart pounding. Sitting back down she placed her hand over her heart to calm herself down.

"Mike, what do you want?"

"I understand your anger, but why are you being so nice to me now?"

"I'm just being civil until we leave the island and we go our separate ways. Then I never what to hear from you again."

"Sad, but I agree. What I did was low, and I don't blame you."

"Good! Now that we understand each other, do you mind refilling my glass?"

"Sure. I can do that, and I'll join you." Mike filled the glasses.

"You know we're running out of wine," said Mike handing Sam her glass.

"We are? Well, we might need a trip into town. I'm sure we're running out of food also. With all our unexpected guests, it stands to reason."

"True. We'll see who wants to go in the morning, right Sam?"

"Right. Good plan. So, tell me. I'm curious if you say that you haven't kept in contact with your boss so to speak, how would they know that we're here on Lanai?"

"That's what I don't understand. Someone else must be working with them."

"And you have no idea who it is?"

"No."

"Unless you're lying, and it's you," smirked Sam

"Me? Sam, I'm—"

"OK. Let's retrace our actions."

"You found the box and your friend Makani was there and others on the team."

"No! It's not Makani! Don't you even go there!"

"I wasn't insinuating it was Makani. Anyway, we went back to your place and what did you do?"

"Well I analyzed the box and called—wait a minute. I called Sue at the lab."

"Was there any other person other than Sue?"

"No, and you were with me when I called Makani."

"Then if it's not Makani that only leaves Sue. She must be working with them. Come to think of it when I made the call at the restaurant, they already knew you had found the box."

"It doesn't make sense. Sue? Really? I can't believe it—I've know her for years. This must be a hell of a big secret for them to go to all this trouble."

"Must be. I honestly can't tell you what it is because they never filled me in on it. My part was to just keep an eye on you and inform them about any significant finds pertaining to the box."

"Oh boy, this is crazy! I never would have expected to be tangled up in this mess."

"I know. It is a mess."

"I wonder where they are and what are they waiting for. They know we're here," said Sam.

"Can't answer that. I really don't know."

"Maybe they want us to reactivate the project before doing away with us."

"Well, with them anything is possible. Peter is your ace in the hole because they don't know anything about him."

"Don't they?"

"No, they don't. And if you're doubtful about that, well Peter made sure I couldn't call them to tell them because he crushed my phone."

"He did? Oh no!" Sam smiled.

"Yeah, he did. He stepped on it and poof! It disintegrated."

"What a good man." Sam and Mike burst into laughter.

Peter and Wally returned. "Aw laughter, now that's good to hear." Peter smiled.

"What's so funny?" asked Wally.

"Oh nothing," laughed Sam.

"Hey guys! Look what I found—a bottle of wine." Peter held up the bottle.

"That's nice we were just mentioning how we're running out of wine and food."

"Good timing then." Peter poured Wally and himself a glass.

"So, in the morning Wally and I can make a run into town," offered Mike.

"Good, then Peter and I can go back to the ship and see what else we can find, right Peter?"

"Right."

"What did you think of the petroglyphs Peter?" asked Sam.

"They certainly gave me something to consider."

"That's for sure. Wally are there any other islands that have as many drawings as this one?"

"I do know that some have been found elsewhere."

"Sam you're an archaeologist, how come you've never looked into this?" asked Mike.

"Good question. I've seen a few, but my main focus are the digs. Going forward, I'll pay more attention to them."

"I think I'll make us a fire." Mike stood up.

"Good idea. I'll help," said Wally.

"I won't be staying up much longer—it's been a full day," said Sam.

"Another full day tomorrow." Peter exchanged seats as Mike stood up.

"It certainly will be."

"Peter, using your telepathy can you tell when we're going to expect company?" asked Sam.

Peter stared off into the distance clearing his mind. "Very soon and I also feel something else."

"Really? What else?"

"Not sure. I can't get a clear image."

"Oh, great! That's just what we need, another surprise!"

Peter smiled. "Yup, and it's a big one that I do know."

"Well then, let's enjoy each other's company for tonight," said Sam.

"Absolutely! Another drink it is."

"You know I'm a little hungry. Let me see if we have any cheese and crackers left." Sam walked over to the cooler.

"What are you looking for Sam?" asked Mike.

"Some cheese and crackers."

"Here, let me help you. There you go."

"Thank you. Oh, I forgot we bought my favorite—Brie." Sam passed the cheese and crackers around.

"Peter."

"Yeah, Mike?"

"What's it like finding your sister alive and well?"

"I couldn't be happier. We have a lot of catching up to do." Peter smiled at Sam.

"We certainly do. And we'll have a lifetime to do it."

"You bet. Here, Wally have some." Peter held out the plate. "Mike, I guess your business with Sam is pretty much over."

"I guess so," said Mike taking a bite.

"Good, then tomorrow when we go into town, you can catch the next boat out."

Mike looked at Sam for a sign of intervention, which didn't come.

"Oh, I thought I was coming back."

"Well, since you're in town why make two trips? You might as well go," said Peter.

"I guess I could do that if you really think that's best."

"Yes," confirmed Peter.

There was an awkward silence and Mike felt that he should call it a night.

"Well, I think I'm going to call it a night."

"OK. See you in the morning."

"Good night Sam." Mike waited for her response before entering his tent.

"Good night Mike." Sam looked around for Wally, but he had already left.

"You know what I think? I'll go too," said Sam. "I'm exhausted."

"Really? I hope it wasn't anything I said?"

"No, don't be silly, Peter. I'm just tired."

"OK, good night then."

Peter watched as Sam walked into her tent. He drank his wine and gazed up at the night sky. Strange he's never seen Mars so close to the Earth before.

TWENTY-SEVEN

PETER TOOK HIS LAST sip of wine and unraveled his sleeping bag. He placed it close to the fire and crawled in. Staring up at the starry night sky it wasn't long before he was fast asleep.

Through the night the wind had picked up sending a chill in the air. He pulled his sleeping bag up around his neck trying to keep warm, which didn't help. He tossed and turned trying to get comfortable, but now there was something besides the wind that was keeping him up.

Frustrated he opened his eyes. The once starry sky was now black as if every star had been extinguished. He stood up wrapping the sleeping bag around his shoulders for warmth. Suddenly it hit—lightning bolts which came fast and furious were hitting the ship. It was not just one but several working in unison with the tremendous gale force. "Sam! Sam!"

Sam awoke with a start, jumped out of her sleeping bag and ran out of the tent.

"What? What? Oh my God!" Sam was quickly

blown back into her tent. Peter pushed his way forward fighting the wind with every step. Sam reemerged from her tent, only to be catapulted to the ground and dragged back into it.

"Sam! Grab my hand." Peter held on to the side of the tent while inserting his arm through the opening. Sam managed to crawl towards the entrance reaching up to grab Peter's hand. Peter pulled her towards him holding on tight for fear that she might be blown away.

Mike and Wally were holding on to a large piece of driftwood for support. Peter and Sam after several tries had managed to reach Mike and Wally, forming a human chain. They watched the spectacle before them.

"What is that?" yelled Sam.

The ship was now engulfed in an orange glow that seemed to be emanating from the sky.

"Peter! What is happening?"

"I don't know! The key must have started the activation."

The glow hovered around the ship for a few moments and then slowly began its ominous descent on to shore.

"It's coming closer," yelled Sam.

Backing up to get out of its path, Wally began chanting prayers in Hawaiian for protection. The orange glow was now changing its shape and forming into a tunnel, pulling in anything in its path.

"Quick! Run!" yelled Peter.

They ran up the beach and into the dense brush.

Jerry couldn't sleep, the dinner at Kō's was fabulous, but he definitely had overindulged. He decided to get some air and walked out to the balcony. Glancing up at the stars, he was surprised when all he saw was blackness. Looking out to the ocean, which was placid, there was a strange orange glow coming from an island off in the distance. He watched as the glow started at one end and was slowly moving up island.

"What is that?" He was awestruck by the light show. Must be fireworks, he assumed. He turned to walk back into the room when he stopped dead in his tracks. He turned to view the light display when the realization hit. "OMG! They did it. SHIT!" Jerry ran into the hallway and pounded on Ramsay's and Andrew's doors.

"What's going on?" asked Ramsay.

"Get your shit together, we're leaving."

Jerry ran back into his room and quickly threw his belongings together. He needed to get to the island in a hurry, he hadn't anticipated that they would figure it out so quickly. Running back out into the hallway, Ramsay and Andrew were ready and waiting.

"Come on let's go!"

"Don't tell me they did it?" said Ramsay as he called for the elevator.

"They did!" exclaimed Jerry.

"It's the middle of the night, how are we going to get there?" asked Ramsay.

"Sir that will pose a bit of a problem. The ferries

aren't scheduled to leave until morning."

"We'll have to find another way. What we could use is a helicopter," said Jerry.

"What? Where?" asked Ramsay. "At this time of night? Where are we going to get a helicopter?"

"We have no other choice but to find one," said Jerry.

Once they reached the lobby they ran to the front desk.

"Can I help you?" asked the young girl.

"Yes, we need to rent a helicopter."

"Oh, a helicopter?"

"Yes," said Jerry.

"Let me check. For what day sir? Can I have your name please?"

"Jerry Talbot and I would like it now!"

"Sir, that's impossible. I can reserve one for you tomorrow morning."

"No, that's not acceptable. I need it now!" said Jerry.

"I'm terribly sorry, Sir, but that's the best I can do."

"Can you settle my bill?"

"Yes, if you would just give me a minute, I'll be right with you."

"Jerry, Jerry," whispered Ramsay "Why are you giving up?"

"Who said I was giving up?"

"Here you go, Sir. This is your total and if you could please sign here."

Jerry signed and handed the papers back to the girl. "Oh, silly me."

"What is it, Sir?"

"I am so embarrassed. I almost forgot to mention this." Jerry looked at Andrew and then leaned on the desk. "You see my friend Gunther Meyer had reserved a helicopter as a surprise birthday gift for our friend over there." Jerry pointed at Andrew. "So, you see we actually do have one reserved."

"Oh, in that case, just let me confirm it. It was reserved by a Gunther Meyer—correct?"

"Yes, that's correct," confirmed Jerry.

"OK. It does seem to have been reserved; just let me print you out a copy of the paperwork. Here you go Sir."

"Good," said Jerry placing the paper into his wallet.

"We can get one of our drivers to take you."

"Thank you. Mahalo. That would be great."

A driver soon appeared and loaded their luggage into the trunk.

"Stop!" yelled Peter. "It's receding back to the beach."

"You're right. I wonder why. Come on, let's follow it," said Sam.

Sam noticed a figure standing with his arms outstretched. As she approached the figure, she recognized him.

"Makani! Makani! What are you doing here?"

Makani remained focused on the orange glow

pushing it back towards the shoreline. Once it was contained, hovering over the ship, Makani lowered his arms.

Sam ran up to Makani. "Makani! I'm so glad to see you."

Sam wrapped her arms around him. "How did you do that? Why are you here?"

"I felt that you might need a little help. Besides I was staying at the Fairmont Kea Lani giving a conference and decided to check up on you."

"I'm so happy you're here—what is that thing?"

"It's an energy vortex, a wormhole used to travel to other planets and galaxies."

"You're absolutely right," said Peter. This is what our father was working on. Sam now can you see the importance of this project? If it were to get into the wrong hands—no telling what purpose it could be used for. They might go so far as to use it for the destruction of other worlds."

"I can see that it could end in global and galactic domination. But how did you control it?" asked Sam.

"Simple, really. All my life I have been a spiritual leader who works on many energy levels and this is just one of them," explained Makani.

"Interesting," said Peter.

"Oh, sorry Peter. I didn't introduce you. This is Makani. Peter."

Makani stared into his eyes for a moment. "Sam's brother."

"Yes, I am but how?"

"I also use telepathy, just as you do."

"I have so many questions, Makani."

Makani placed his arm around Sam. "I know my dear Sam, but all of your questions will be answered shortly. All I will tell you is that these islands have a very strong mana and I and several other spiritual leaders have taken a sacred vow to teach all those who are open to the sacred energies of Aloha. It's our way of life, our law that we wholeheartedly welcome as part of who we are."

"It's a law?" asked Mike.

"Yes, our only law that is rightfully destined. A law of love and respect for all, including non human entities. When your heart and mind are open to respecting and seeing all life as one working in unison that's when you can truly understand the importance of all life."

"So, there is life elsewhere?"

"More than you will ever know. Once you understand and let go of all fears anything that's deemed as different will cease to be an obstruction for love and understanding. We and other worlds must coexist as a whole."

"Fascinating," said Wally.

"So, what does this orange beam have to do with anything?" asked Mike.

"Well, it looks like you have just reopened a communication channel."

"Reopened? You mean it was here before?" asked Mike.

"Years ago," said Makani.

"Is that the fire that our legends talk about?" asked Wally.

"Yes, but enough with the questions. They're here. I need your help," said Makani.

"Help? How can we help?" asked Peter.

"Peter, you know what needs to be done."

"I do?" said Peter puzzled.

"Yes, you do. Now think. Here let me help you." Makani stood beside Peter, facing the glow. Eyes closed, they stretched out their arms with palms facing up. Sam stood close to Mike and Wally for support, uncertain what would happen next. Suddenly the orange ball of light began to rotate, accelerating its speed and exposed a dark tunnel at its center. It remained stationary as if waiting for something.

"That was a good one Jerry. How did you know?"

"It pays to be social," replied Jerry.

"There they are!" yelled Ramsay from the seat of the helicopter.

"Yeah, I see them. Can you land here?" Jerry pointed to a clearing that was perfect.

The pilot banked to the right finding a safe spot and prepared to land. Once on the ground Jerry jumped out of the helicopter ducking down from the whirling blades.

"Hurry!" Jerry ran towards the beach, closely

followed by Ramsay and Andrew.

"Peter look! They're here! Now what do we do?"

Peter looked at Makani and understood what needed to be done.

"Sam come here." Peter held out his hand. "How much do you trust me?"

"You're my brother, and I trust you without question."

"Good then here hold my hand and hold on tight—tighter than you've ever held on."

Sam reluctantly reached for his hand, and they walked down to the shoreline. The wind gusts were steadily increasing.

"Sam! What are you doing? Stop!" Mike ran down, trying to pull her away from Peter.

"Mike stop! It's OK. I need to do this! Let go!"

"No, I can't let you go! It's dangerous! What if it kills you?" pleaded Mike.

"I'll be fine. I need to go. I understand now."

"Sam, understand what?"

"I can't explain. I just know I'll be all right."

"I want you to know that I never meant to hurt you."

"Peter give me a minute."

"OK, but hurry," urged Peter.

"Mike, I know deep down that you didn't mean to hurt me and I want you to know that I still love you. You were the only man in my life."

"Sam, do you mean that?"

"Yes, I do. So please remember that."

"Sam, I've loved you from the first time we met, and I will always love you."

Sam leaned into Mike and they exchanged a passionate kiss. "Goodbye Mike."

Sam rejoined Peter and reaching for his hand they continued to walk towards the rotating tunnel.

"Stop!" yelled Jerry, as he ran down the beach. Mike watched as Peter and Sam walked to the water's edge. An extension of the tunnel protruded outward lifting their bodies up into its mouth. In an instant they were gone.

"Sam! No!" cried Mike

TWENTY-EIGHT

SAM AND PETER WATCHED from above as Mike, Makani and Wally were joined by three other men. Their images quickly disappeared as they were hurled into the abyss. Sam held on tightly to Peter's hand, afraid of losing him.

They were in a large tunnel that was illuminated with a brilliant transparent blue light. She could see stars forming and exploding; it was magnificent. It felt like she was suspended in warm water, calming, but her breathing felt labored and she held her breath.

When she couldn't hold it any longer, she slowly started to inhale and exhale, which forced her to relax. Surprisingly, the tunnel had an ample amount of oxygen. She could see a small red planet off in the distance, which was becoming increasingly larger.

It was only a matter of seconds before they were now on the planet itself. Still encased in the tube, which had served as a protective barrier, they were unable to exit.

She watched as it automatically attached itself on

to a larger transparent tunnel that was situated in a mountain ridge. Sam was still holding Peter's hand until the connection was complete.

"Peter, I don't feel very well." Sam could feel her legs beginning to give away.

"Sam!" Peter grabbed her before she collapsed.

"Sam, take deep breaths. Listen to me, take deep breaths!"

"No….I'm…" Sam felt disorientated.

"Listen to me! Take deep breaths! You'll be all right."

Sam took small breaths at first and then a deeper breath. She could feel herself regaining her energy.

"Are you OK?" asked Peter, who was gently rubbing her back.

"Yes, I think so."

"Good girl, come on." Peter lifted her to her feet.

"Peter, where are we? I want to go home. I don't like this place."

"Me neither. Let's see if we can find a way out."

Peter sensed something but was not sure what it was. He released his grip on Sam.

"Peter, don't let go of me!" begged Sam.

"Here. Hang on!" He reached for her hand, wiping his hand dry from her sweat.

They walked along the tube which had a gelatinous consistency making their steps buoyant. Peter guided Sam to the side of the tube.

"Peter, no! Don't touch it!" exclaimed Sam.

"Sam, it's OK," reassured Peter.

But to Peter it really wasn't OK. He was just as scared as Sam but didn't want to admit it. He cautiously placed his hands on to the surface walls, which seemed to be made of the same substance as the floor but was ice cold to the touch. Peter rubbed his hands together for warmth.

"Sam come here. Feel this."

Sam slowly walked over. "I really don't want to," she said nervously.

"Here, give me your hand."

Sam approached the wall apprehensively.

"It feels gelatinous," said Sam and quickly withdrew her hand from Peter's grasp. "It feels like jelly."

"Yes, exactly."

Peter peered outside. "Look we can view the landscape! The colors look like our deserts on Earth."

"You're right, it does. I have this strange urge to just burst out of this tube and run outside."

"You better not, but I know what you mean. It feels familiar."

"Let's see where this tunnel leads."

Sam followed Peter as they walked cautiously through the tube.

"Do you think anyone is here?" whispered Sam.

"I believe so. I'm getting some thought transference, but I'm not sure where it's coming from."

"You are?"

"The strange thing is that I feel it's non-threatening."

"I hope you're right."

Sam was still reluctant to believe it.

They walked for what seemed like miles until they came to an entrance that was deeply imbedded into the mountain.

"Now what? Are we going in?" asked Sam.

"It looks like there's a room up ahead."

"Let's go. Sam watch your step!" cautioned Peter.

Sam stepped carefully over the raised surface. They were now descending into the mountain.

"How far down do you think we are?"

"I don't know—several feet for sure. Hey look."

Ahead of them was a large room filled with consoles and a window that was blacked out. Peter could sense that they were not alone.

"Hello? Is anyone here?" called Peter. Sam grabbed on to the back of Peter's shirt.

"Sam look over there," pointed Peter.

They noticed a large console where a shadowy cloaked figure was seated.

"Peter…. what's that?" Sam dug her nails into Peter's side.

"Ouch!"

"Sorry." She released her nails, but not her grip.

"It looks like we're about to meet our hosts."

The figure was joined by another. They were dressed in brown cloaks resembling monks on Earth.

Their appearance was somewhat humanoid. Tall slender beings with large deep set oval eyes blue in color, large noses comparable to a parakeets. Their skin was white with a bluish tinge that gave off an effervescent glow.

Their appendages were long and slender. As they moved, they seemed to glide effortlessly almost as if they were levitating. One of the beings—possibly the leader wore a royal blue star that was pinned on the left side of his cloak. He had now turned his attention to Peter.

"Here, I'll try and communicate with them telepathically," said Peter focusing his thoughts. To his surprise the figure had abruptly replied to his question.

"You are on Mars."

"Why are we here?" continued Peter with his unspoken dialogue.

"You have been selected as the chosen ones who will help us."

"Help you? How?"

"In time you will know."

"Peter, are you talking to him or is it she?" asked Sam.

"Yes, I am a male."

The figure looked over at Sam, and she quickly reached for Peter's hand as he glided over towards her. He raised his arm and extended his three fingers, one of which was now radiating a blue light. Sam backed up trying to avoid the blue light that was now positioned in the middle of her forehead.

"What are you doing? Leave her alone," cried Peter, trying to shield Sam from his touch.

The entity lowered his arm.

"What did you do to her?"

"I just made our communication less difficult by enhancing her telepathic abilities."

"Sam can you hear me?" asked Peter telepathically.

"Yes, I can and I can hear him too." Sam was astonished by her new ability to communicate.

"There is nothing to fear, fear is but a useless human emotion," said the entity as he glided towards the console.

"Don't be afraid Sam. He won't hurt us."

"Easy to say. I'll work on that. What do they want with us?"

"He wants us to help them," said Peter.

"Help them? How are we going to do that? We can't even help ourselves to get out of here."

"You will know in time, once you receive all the information," replied the entity.

"Come, there is something I would like you to see."

Sam and Peter walked over towards the console.

"What is your name?" asked Sam.

"I am Olos and he is Laton."

"Olos and Laton. Interesting names."

Laton was identical to Olos with only a few exceptions in his outward appearance. He was much shorter and did not wear the ornamental star. He never spoke but only obeyed. They showed no emotion, but they were caring in a gentle way. Olos placed his wispy hand on Laton's shoulder as he gave his order.

"Come Laton, active the console."

Laton swiped his long willowy figures over the controls. The large black screen suddenly came to life.

"Peter look! It's the Earth!" Sam was amazed by the enormity of the image that filled the entire screen.

"Yes, it is," confirmed Olos.

"What do you want with Earth?" asked Peter.

Olsos did not answer; he just turned towards the screen. Suddenly there were several rings that appeared around the Earth. One was red which soon dissipated, then a blue that also dissipated and finally a gold.

"What does this mean?" asked Peter.

"Watch," said Olos.

Another planet appeared beside Earth.

"What planet is that? Mars?" asked Sam.

Olos nodded.

"Are we seeing this at the present?" asked Peter who was overwhelmed by the image.

"No this is the past," said Olos.

"Mars looks exactly like Earth." Peter was astonished. "Sam do you believe this?"

"I see it, but I don't believe it," said Sam who was mesmerized by the similarity.

"It's amazing to think that Mars was once earth like. What happened?" asked Peter.

"You will see; continue watching."

Peter and Sam were enthralled by what they saw

next. A large explosion emanated from Earth that rippled throughout space encompassing the Earth. The rings began to form, then disappeared. A planet which they assumed was indeed Mars had now morphed into a desolate red planet. Peter and Sam turned towards each other; they couldn't believe what they had just witnessed.

"Olos, I hope this isn't true, tell me it's not." Olos did not respond.

"Peter are you thinking what I'm thinking? There's just no way!" exclaimed Sam.

"Sam, I'm afraid so. We destroyed their planet."
Olos said nothing.

"No, that's impossible!" Peter turned towards Sam.

"Did we?" asked Sam staring at Olos.

"It was what you call a nuclear bomb. Sadly, the effects of your testing had destroyed several key areas on Earth that enable us to travel directly to your planet through what you know as wormholes. One of the blasts traveled directly to this planet, such as you, and destroyed our planet's surface."

"Do you know what this means? We unknowingly destroyed life in a futile attempt for what purpose?" Peter slapped his fist into his hand, trying to contain his anger.

"For domination!" sighed Sam. "A useless trait."

"So tell me what happened to your civilization?"

"We could foresee the impending destruction and we constructed these chambers that you see now. Your planet and ours had a symbiotic relationship, meaning our life forms and yours had always cohabited in harmony. Several of our life forms have chosen to remain on Earth and in turn humans have also remained with us."

"Then it was you who had accomplished several of our architectural wonders of the day," commented Sam

"Yes, we did assist," replied Olos.

"Where on Earth do you call home?" asked Peter.

"We had chosen what you call the Hawaiian Islands as home."

"Why?" asked Sam.

"The terrain and climate are much like our beloved Mars. When we first arrived, we were not feared by the inhabitants. They had accepted us and understood our spiritual love of all things. This is truly embedded in our way of life," explained Olos.

"Let me get this straight—the Hawaiian ways stem from your culture?" asked Sam.

"Yes, we are all one."

"That's beautiful. The islands do have a magical spell that captures your inner being."

"Yes, but unfortunately only a few chosen beings understand its true essence."

"That's strange—that is exactly what Makani has been saying," said Sam.

"Are there other life forms on Earth from other planets?" asked Peter.

"Yes, there are many," replied Olos.

"Who are the others? And where are they from?"

Laton waved his hand over the console. The screen lit up, displaying a large black hole. They watched as ships emerged from within and sped to Earth.

"They come from different galaxies and have also populated your Earth."

"Who are they?" asked Peter.

"Some are a war like people called Bellators."

"Bellator? Why does that name sound so familiar?" asked Sam. "Oh, I remember Peter, it's Latin for warrior."

"Interesting."

"We approached your government and expressed our concerns; however, they made promises with us that they neglected to keep."

"What promises?" asked Sam.

"That you will find out at a later date. We have taken it upon ourselves to protect Earth from the Bellator by intercepting their spacecrafts in another dimension. You cannot see the intervention.

"Is that why we on Earth have spotted objects from time to time?" asked Peter.

"Yes, we do show ourselves at times, but this is not our intension. We would rather keep the deflection hidden."

"So, if you could travel to Earth in your ships, then why is the wormhole of such importance?" asked Peter.

"Its importance is not one for our beings, but its importance is for you as humans as a mode of travel.

You're still learning, and it is in your future."

"Was our father involved in anyway? We believe that he was working for the government," asked Sam.

"At first he was working for your government, until we made contact. We enlightened him of our situation and how we were in need of his assistance. Primarily to activate wormholes as needed for transportation. He had also discovered a device that would enable your oxygen to be available at the time of transportation," explained Olos.

"So that's why we could breathe," said Peter.

"Yes. He had accomplished the task. Your father was a great man and he agreed with our terms to represent our planet."

"I can't believe that! It's incredible. But why?" asked Peter.

"We need humans to speak for us, and to communicate to your government the dire dangers that Earth faces."

"Dangers?"

"Yes, many. You will learn if you choose to stay," added Olos.

"I don't know what we should do Peter?"

"You are free to go at any time you choose," said Olos. "We have much knowledge to share and prepare you for our mission."

"I would like to discuss this with Sam," said Peter.

"Yes, by all means." Olos nodded at Laton. They both left the room.

"Peter, what are we going to do?"

"Well, I know what I need to do."

"And what's that?" Sam looked deep into Peter's eyes. "Peter, no! Really?"

"Sam, I want to help them."

"Do you really believe everything he's saying?"

"It's hard not to. If our father was working with them, then I'm sure they can be trusted. Sam I'm staying—if you don't want to, I understand."

"Peter! No! Please don't," begged Sam.

"Sam look, he did say we had the option to leave at any time. What's the harm in staying? We could learn so much from them."

"If you put it that way, I am a little curious about what they can teach us."

"So for now let's stay?"

Sam paused for a moment and then walked around the room.

"OK, fine we'll stay, but let's make sure we can leave when we want to."

"I will. Sam this is going to be an exciting experience."

"I'm sure it will be."

Peter was ready to call Olos, but he had already entered the room.

"We can leave whenever we want?" asked Peter, staring at Sam.

"Yes, most definitely," said Olos.

"OK, we'll stay."

Olos nodded and raised his hands. He was joined by two more beings.

"We will show you your accommodations."

Sam followed Peter as they were led out of the control room.

"Olos, just one question," asked Peter. "How are we going to help you?"

"You will be trained to be our ambassadors just like your father. We will work together to help your kind to evolve and to restore your Earth to its natural state."

"And what state is that?" asked Sam.

"The state of ALOHA!"